To Patsy

Such a l

and genuine person

Best wishes,

Will x

C000061217

Mister Nice

THE NOVEL

Will Templeton

Interior Layout by Textual Eyes
Design for Print Services

Acknowledgements

The journey to this point for Mister Nice and his cast of characters has been an unusual one, for myself and, I dare say, for any writer. Initially a very short one-act play written for friends to read, it was then developed into a full-length play, first performed at the Doncaster Little Theatre in November 2022. From there came the inspiration to turn it into this modest novel (novel/novella? Some sources say anything over 40k word count is classed as a novel, so I'm going with that) which you now hold in your hands.

I miss the good old days of the writing group, when Tommy Savage, Jade-Lee Saxelby, Will Tollerfield, Danny Glover and I used to try to out-write one another, and I miss the banter and mutual encouragement.

I'm grateful to my theatre colleagues and the cast of the stage production of the play, notably Chris Bolus, David Chambers, Robert Mee, Claire Ramos, Alan Clark, Grace Cundy and Neil Snowdon, for bringing the characters to life, to great critical acclaim.

I'd like to extend special thanks to the readers who have seen all or part of earlier drafts and given me their two-pen'orth, namely Kath Middleton, Samantha Brownley, Samantha Constantine, Steve Munoz, Mike Hemming, Amanda Pope and Nikola Symołon. Any remaining errors, either factual or typographical, are entirely ~~their fault for not being sharper~~ my own.

Also by Will Templeton

Novels
(Maxey and Preston series)

Births, Marriages and Death
Tie the Knot

Anthology, as co-editor/contributor

Criminal Shorts

Plays, available for reading or performance

No Harm Done
Jenny's Friend
Another Bite
Sod's Law
Splish Splash
Comings and Goings
Taboo
Her Smile
Mister Nice (the stage play)

For permission to perform any of these plays
please contact: willtempleton@outlook.com

Book One

Richard Kirkwood

Chapter One

'Damn it!' Richard Kirkwood swore, hurling the heavy book across the room. He immediately rushed across and retrieved it, checking for damage and replacing it delicately onto his desk.

He picked up the candle which had been knocked over in his outburst, using a taper to take a flame from another to relight it. He then returned the candle to its position on the floor, at one of the points of the star he had chalked upon his floorboards.

He looked around him, satisfying himself that all was as it had been, and as it should be. The pentacle, with its arcane symbols drawn assiduously around the circle's edge, copied meticulously from the book. The candles, black as obsidian, one at each of the five points. The crystals, arranged amongst the symbols. The incense burning in each corner of the room.

'Richard?'

His wife knocked on the door, rattled the handle.

'Is everything all right? I heard you call out.'

'Everything is fine, Grace,' he said, voice raised to be heard through the thick oak. He made no attempt to unlock the door. 'There's nothing to worry yourself over. I merely dropped... something.'

'If you're sure...'

'Quite sure, my dear.'

He moved from the door, the interruption already forgotten, though it was a few moments before his wife's footsteps retreated along the hallway.

Kirkwood took a deep breath, tucked his thumbs into the pockets of his waistcoat and organised his thoughts. The required items were in place. He checked the book once more to ensure he had the necessary passage visible before him, the alien wording showing clearly on the open page.

Was it too early? Night was the ideal time for business such as this to be conducted, everyone knew that. Distractions from other members of the household were minimised, and the powers that he was attempting to contact were more receptive by moonlight, more willing to respond.

But he was so impatient! Even though he had been working on this task for many months, he felt that his endeavours were drawing to a close, that the culmination of his immense undertaking was at hand. So long had he pursued this dream, he felt it had been his life's sole compulsion. Fellow students and his tutors and professors had shunned him and looked condescendingly at his academic preferences. But he turned his back on them all, on the whole world, concentrating on his vision. Now, finally his efforts would be rewarded.

And what rewards he dreamed of!

Power unheard of in the realms of mortal men. Wealth and dominion beyond even his engorged ambitions. All within his grasp. If only he could make that last connection...

Was it his pronunciation? The words inscribed in the antique tome were strange indeed. No lips of man had spoken them in living memory. Perhaps the symbols were not transcribed as accurately as he had hoped. Chalk was not an ideal tool, the floorboards rough and uneven. The designs were intricate and the pages of the book were worn and faded in places, making them difficult to decipher.

The book itself was ancient beyond understanding. Its very existence threatened man's concept of human history. Passed from hand to shadowy hand over the centuries, hidden from the world at large, its contents spoken of only in whispers, the secret of its power guarded gravely and jealously.

He had learned of the book from a man who dared not even show his face, whose pseudonym had been told to him from an acquaintance at the bookstore he frequented, who knew of him from a friend who had another friend who knew of a secret coven which congregated deep in the woods outside the town where yet another friend resided. This man had met Kirkwood wearing a mask and hood to conceal his features, and even then his furtive eyes flicked constantly towards the door and windows of the backstreet dive where their rendezvous took place, his head turning to peer over his shoulder at the slightest sound or movement.

Queen Victoria's golden jubilee celebrations had the whole nation joined in joyous festivity, the populace thronged the streets in merriment, yet these two huddled in the dark and talked of sinister things.

Kirkwood would have paid far more than the man asked for the precious tome, but the mysterious stranger had seemed keen to pass it on, as if eager to relieve himself of its possession. Kirkwood dismissed such fears and negativity, desperate to feel the cracked leather cover with his own hands, and to run his fingers over the stiff, crumbling parchment of the pages.

Hopes that its enigmas would quickly be revealed to his enquiries were soon dashed, as it steadfastly refused to offer up its knowledge. He conjectured that maybe he had been swindled, and that the book had been fabricated for the sole purpose of duping the unwary. But the modest purchase price and the obvious age of the materials involved in the construction of the item immediately put such thoughts out of his mind.

Besides, the book itself exuded an energy, a force, which could not be counterfeited. The sheer presence of it told of the immense power contained within. There it sat on his desk even now, between the skulls and the statuettes of dark gods and devils, like a manifestation of supremacy and control.

If only he could unlock its mysteries.

Kirkwood drew the thick curtains, blocking out the day, and turned up the mantle on the wall above his desk, just enough to illuminate the text scrawled across the brittle pages. He affixed his *pince nez* to the bridge of his broad nose and squinted at the scratchy writing. He licked his dry lips and concentrated on the words, forming them in his mind before he set them to his tongue. He practiced them at a mumble, rolling them around his mouth, then, when he felt he was ready, he spoke them aloud.

'*Maz sharat sha mashaz alamdak. Mushu maz sharat alash.*'

He held his breath and waited, listening, searching the darkest shadows of the room. No answer came from the gloom, so he repeated the invocation, his voice louder, firmer: '*Maz sharat sha mashaz alamdak. Mushu maz sharat alash.*'

Silence. Stillness.

Again, with growing fervour: '*Maz sharat sha mashaz alamdak. Mushu maz sharat alash!*'

The silence continued. The stillness remained undisturbed.

'Hell and damnation!'

The book hurtled across the room once more, and again the hurried chase followed to rescue it from his ill-treatment, checking the spine, ensuring the pages were still intact. With a sigh of utmost frustration and despair he blew out the candles and returned the book to his desk.

Kirkwood sat in his chair, removed his glasses, rested his forehead upon the book, and wept.

*

Closing the huge door behind him, Kirkwood skipped down the steps to the street. He brushed down the lapels of his frock coat and tilted the brim of his top hat against the sun. He felt Grace's presence at the bay window, her eyes on his back, and he steadfastly avoided her gaze. He knew she cared, he knew she worried about his interests, his 'fixation' as she called it, but he couldn't allow her concerns to distract him. Not when he was this close to achieving his dreams.

The high, broad frontages of Grosvenor Street towered either side of the wide thoroughfare as he strode the pavement, silver-tipped cane swinging at his side. A hansom trundled by, led by a tall chestnut steed. Two ladies walked along the opposite side of the road, their bustles swaying in their wake, parasols shielding their pale skin from the day's glare, gloves and bonnets worn as protection against the cool spring breeze. Otherwise the street was his alone.

He allowed his feet their freedom, venturing off Grosvenor until he found himself amidst the flawlessly trimmed lawns of Mount Street Gardens. He took a seat on one of the benches, enjoyed the snowdrops in the borders, the squirrels hopping on the branches above his head, until he spied the tall windows of the Catholic Church of the Immaculate Conception peering down at him through the trees. He felt the disapproval emanating from the stained glass eyes, saw the disdain in the curled lip of the high arches, and with a shudder he left his perch and walked on.

All around him was clean and bright, and he felt soiled and sullied, a pus-swollen blemish on the fresh cheek of Mayfair. It occurred to him that location might be a factor in the impediments to the success of his labours. Might the sheer cleanliness of his surroundings deter a tarnished soul from venturing here? Would less salubrious quarters be more welcoming?

He tapped his cane on the path decisively and turned his step towards home.

Chapter Two

'Don't worry, love,' said the lean, hard-faced woman. 'It's easy. Just get the first one under your belt, so to speak, and you'll never look back.'

Clara Stobbs nodded and tried to move away, but the older woman had more wisdom to impart.

'Been working these streets for years now,' Ada Eccles continued. 'Best place to find a likely bloke is near a pub, like the Frying Pan or the Britannia. They comes out o' them places horny and tiddly, and looking for a warm skirt to shove their cold 'ands under.'

Clara curled a tentative smile, showing that most of her teeth were still present, and not too discoloured by tobacco and her meagre diet. Ada's eager grin reminded the younger woman of the path beneath their feet, brown and gritty and half the cobbles missing.

'I wouldn't be out here at this time of night,' Clara said, tugging her worn and faded shawl tight around her shoulders, 'only my ol' man's lost 'is job and there's four little mouths crying for their dinners.'

Ada wafted a dismissive hand.

'We've all got a sob story, lass. None of us would be out 'ere looking for business if we 'ad the choice. See Mary Ann down there?'

She pointed along the dark street where the flickering flame of a street lamp cast a hazy halo in the heavy fog. A figure turned in the dim light, twirling her hem and looking this way and that, trying to catch the eye of any passing gentlemen.

'Nanny in a fancy household, she were,' Ada tutted, 'until the brats' mummy comes 'ome unexpected, like, and catches her hubby with Mary Ann over his knee, treating her like a naughty girl, if you know what I mean.'

She shook her head and rolled her eyes.

'There's Mary Ann expecting a few pennies extra in her pay packet and instead she gets the boot, without a reference to show to the next household she tried.'

'That's awful,' Clara said.

'Is it?' Ada sneered. 'Least she's seen the inside of a decent gaff. Most o' the girls along these streets have been in the gutter since birth, and spread their legs for thruppence to pay for a place in the doss house, just so they don't 'ave to bed down in someone's privy.'

'Privy?'

'If they're lucky.'

She shrugged her bony shoulders.

'Better that stink than being stuck out on the street with the rain pissing down and the chill biting through your drawers.'

Clara took a step closer and lowered her voice. 'How did you know, anyway?'

'What? That it were yer first time?'

Ada laughed, a wet, raspy cackle that culminated in a fit of coughing. She hoiked a glob of phlegm into the road.

'Jittery little mouse like you? You didn't know where to look when you tottered up the path. First bloke what eyed you up, I thought you was going to wet yourself.'

Clara felt the colour flood her cheeks.

'There's no shame in trying to provide for your family, love. Queen Vickie 'as sat there in her grand palace, all comfy-cosy on her cushioned throne for fifty years, with no idea what it's like for the real people out 'ere in the real world. She don't know the squalor and grime we 'ave to put up with. You can bet she's never short of a nip o' gin to 'elp 'er get through the night without the shivers. And there's all those lah-de-dah folks over the other side of the city, with their theatres and their rest'rants who don't give a tuppenny fart about what's 'appening in the East End. There's more people crammed into these few streets than in 'alf the rest of the bloody country! The slums are heavin' with the 'opeless and the 'elpless, with no jobs and no futures. The Jews are floodin' in from Europe and we're already six to a room in most houses round 'ere, and that's not counting the rats.'

Clara felt the colour drain from her cheeks.

'Sorry, darlin',' Ada said, sweeping an arm around her shoulder and drawing her in close. 'I do go on, don't I?'

Clara strained not to wince at the stench of body odour and cheap liquor emanating from the woman.

'My dear, sweet old muvvah, gawd rest 'er soul, allus used to say I was cursed with 'alf a brain,' Ada continued, 'which was a quarter more'n most folks round 'ere.'

She cackled and coughed.

Once freed from the other's grasp Clara straightened her shawl and jutted a proud chin.

'You're right,' she said. 'No shame. If the powers what be ain't going to look after us, we've got to look after ourselfs.'

'That's the spirit, lass,' Ada said, giving Clara a gentle punch on the arm. 'Now, drop your drawers and grab a man!'

With a last laugh and splutter at Clara's shocked expression, Ada turned and shuffled off into the darkness and smog, reappearing briefly as she exchanged a word with Mary Ann beneath the gaslight of the street corner lamp, before vanishing once more into shadow.

As the scuff of Ada's footsteps faded and the gloom of the post-midnight hours fell heavy on her shoulders, Clara felt more alone than she ever had. Though Mary Ann still strutted only yards away, and the thrum and throb of raucous music and laughter swept along the street every time a customer opened the door of the Ten Bells just a short way along Fournier Street, Clara imagined herself exiled and exposed far from any other human life. How could it be that she stood here now, vulnerable and afraid on this filthy street? How John Stobbs, who promised to love and care for her always, could allow her out into the night like this was staggering beyond belief. Oh, he'd asked her if she was sure there was no other way, and he'd lowered his eyes as she'd pinched rouge into her cheeks and adjusted her corset, but he'd not stood firm in the doorway and barred her exit. He'd not steered her back to her rightful place in the kitchen and sworn all would be well, he'd find other work, he'd see them right, he would provide. No, he'd held open the door, offered her an insipid smile obviously intended as encouraging, even patted her shoulder as she stepped past him into the engulfing night, the shilling or two that she might return home with clearly more important to him than his pride. Than her dignity.

More important even than her safety. The crime rates on these dark, filthy streets were a crime in themselves. The East End had been largely forgotten by the authorities. Ada was right. While the West End prospered the East End sank further into the mire of its bleak existence. Even with spring waning the residents hereabouts had little expectation of feeling the sun on their faces any time soon. Clara had seen a snowdrop thrust up its tiny white head between the cracked cobbles a few days ago, though its pitiful lifespan beneath the thousands of feet tramping back and forth had been briefer than the weak smile the memory brought to her lips. What hope was there for anything frail, having to suffer the harsh conditions present in this part of London, in the year of our Lord, 1888?

The click-clack of well-made heels on the cracked pavement alerted Clara to the approach of a heavyset gentleman, top-hat throwing thick shadow over his face. She glanced along the street – the haze beneath the gas lamp on the corner was currently unoccupied. Mary Ann must have left on some other man's arm while Clara was pondering the grim thoughts that Ada's rambling had raised in her mind. The man shortened his stride, lingering close by Clara, hidden eyes considering her, gloved fingers stroking a bearded chin thoughtfully.

With a deep breath to steel her nerves Clara held out a shaky hand to him. After a moment he accepted the gesture, placing his palm in hers and following Clara into the even deeper gloom of a nearby alley.

'You'll have to forgive me if I'm a bit 'esitant,' Clara said. 'I've never done this before.'

And she gingerly set about loosening her clothing.

'That's all right,' said Jack, slipping a bundle

from the pocket of the silk frock coat and unwrapping the sharp blade. 'You're my first one, too.'

Chapter Three

'Have you missed me, Kirkwood?'

Kirkwood gasped, startled, and turned his gaze to the large chair by the cold hearth. A moment before it had been unoccupied.

'Surprised to see me?' asked the shadowy figure seated there. 'You called me here.'

Kirkwood coughed and cleared a throat hoarse from the hours spent repeating the chants and mantras he had learned from the book he clutched before him.

'You're resisting me,' he said.

'Surely you can't fault me for wishing to extend my freedom as long as possible?'

The figure appeared relaxed as it lounged, cross-legged, but there was a tension in the way its long fingers curled around the arms of the chair which belied the ease it attempted to convey.

Night had crept into the room during the long period of his labours, swallowing the area beyond Kirkwood's desk in its heavy gloom, but he was not tempted to light more mantles. He had no desire to better observe his guest.

This chamber was darker, more dank and dreary, than his study in the big house across the city. The building was smaller but still comprised of several rooms spread over two floors, space that was overrun with poor people before he had it cleared and renovated. But still a hint of the former squalor remained, exuding from the walls. The desperation and desolation of the lost and fearful had seeped into the fabric of the building itself, making it a far more suitable receptacle for the being he had summoned than the splendour of Mayfair, just a handful of miles distant.

Here in Bethnal Green the conditions had proven ideal for his purposes, though hardly ideal for the neighbouring residents who swarmed like ants on the streets beyond his barricaded doors. It was their despair which attracted the thing that stared at him now with eyes that glinted malevolently, even in these dim surroundings. Eyes that could charm and bedazzle if one held their gaze too long.

Eyes that had indeed mesmerised the naïve fool who yearned for so long to make contact with the realms beyond imagining. When the tall, striking figure first appeared in the chalk circle, naked and arrogant, Kirkwood had been stunned. Where was the horned, fanged, snarling, cursing monstrosity he had been expecting? This was a man in all aspects, and one of fine, classical stature.

Awestruck, Kirkwood approached the stranger, walking around the circle, examining him with a wide stare and a slack jaw, his brain abuzz with excitement.

'What is it you desire?' the rich, deep voice purred.

Kirkwood opened his mouth to utter banalities such as wealth and power, the ostensible purpose behind his relentless campaign, but the words died on his lips. In those piercing eyes he saw reflected all that lay hidden deep within himself, the secret inspirations and aspirations, dreads and cravings that led him to this. He saw his father's back, turned to him so very often; his mother's hands passing him to the nanny while she took succour from her numerous ailments with liberal doses of laudanum; his wife's frown as her clothes lay on the floor but his manhood remained dormant; the downcast eyes of the fresh-faced footman, whose earthy musk had stirred his unspoken passion, as he packed his bags and left their employ.

The deep, barren hole in his chest was a frozen landscape from whence his shrivelled heart cried out from its icy prison. Kirkwood took a moment to regain his breath before he allowed his tongue to form the answer to the stranger's question. An answer which surprised him more than his visitor. Which clawed its way from his reluctant mouth with angry talons.

'Love,' he gasped.

And the stranger stepped from the circle and took him in its arms.

*

'Where were you?'

'Oh, just strolling,' the thing said. 'Taking in the sights of the slums.'

It inhaled deeply.

'Drinking in the stench of the streets.'

'Is that all?' Kirkwood peered keenly into the shadows. Was that blood the creature licked from its fingers with a flickering tongue?

'I may have discovered a new hobby,' came the drawling, sardonic reply.

'Hobby?' Kirkwood scoffed. 'It cannot be anything pleasant to entertain one such as yourself.'

'On the contrary,' the other said, 'I found it most pleasant and eminently entertaining.'

'Do you intend to disclose the manner of this pastime?'

'Not presently, but I am sure that you will learn of it in due course.'

'That does not bode well for the denizens of the streets beyond these walls.'

'Perhaps not.'

Silence settled, broken only by the rich tick-tick-ticking of the grandfather clock in the corner, purchased by Kirkwood to add a touch of normality, of humanity, to the eerie chamber.

With a chuckle the creature rose from its seat and arched its back, stretching its arms high, turning its head left and right to ease its neck. Kirkwood watched it looming high above him, fearing it would not stop upon reaching the ceiling, and that it would crash through into the attic space, affecting an escape by these means.

The creature recognised his concern. 'Fear not, Kirkwood,' it said. 'I am safely returned to captivity within this metal cage you have designed.' It winced as the toe of its ornately buckled boot nudged the heavy chain which encircled the chair from which it had recently risen. The base iron of the links formed an effective restraint to any eldritch being caught within, and the enchantments that Kirkwood had gleaned from the ancient grimoire he so treasured had multiplied its efficacy incalculably.

'Though the closeness of the barricade is somewhat claustrophobic.'

It rolled its shoulders and emitted a low growl through curled lips. The numerous hours it had spent in that tiny enclosure, prior to its recent sojourn, became quite irksome to it.

'Would that you had remained so confined

this entire time,' Kirkwood said grimly.

'And so I should have, had you not attempted to dismiss me from this plane of existence.'

The thing laughed, a harsh, rasping breath.

'Your command of the incantation required is distinctly lacking.'

Kirkwood squirmed in his seat. His efforts to return the creature whence he had summoned it were disastrous, instead causing its release. His carelessness had left it free to roam the city at will, whilst Kirkwood frantically sought to retrieve it, as eventually he had. Its exploits in the intervening hours were thus far a mystery; a mystery to which he dreaded uncovering the solution.

*

Initially Kirkwood had been delighted at what he had summoned. The being offered relief from his solitude without the guilt or shame associated with such closeness. Intimacy without attachment.

The limits of the thing's precincts had been achieved by barring the windows and welding iron to the door of the study. Such other liberty Kirkwood had allowed it, ensuring not to leave the grimoire in the room when he was not in attendance, for fear of the creature gaining its independence by its own means. It had so insinuated itself into his good graces that he considered extending the borders further, until the chambermaid he employed to maintain the rooms, though having strict orders to avoid entry to the study, went suddenly missing without explanation. Though the creature denied any knowledge of the girl's fate, thenceforth

Kirkwood limited its movements and bound it to the chair.

His grim suspicions grew within him, and he finally sought to repulse the creature from this human realm into which he himself had summoned it. It was then he came to realise his ghastly mistake. The requisite incantations eluded him. The pages of the book retained their riddles, keeping from him the necessary phrases to achieve his new aim. Frustration at being so thwarted prompted Kirkwood into carelessness, thus releasing the being upon the unsuspecting city.

As the one who had brought forth the demon Kirkwood himself was safe from its wrath, but he could not guess what havoc it might wreak upon the people it found in the streets beyond these walls. Hence his fraught but ultimately successful exertions to restore it to its place within the circle of chains.

'I must say,' the creature said, regaining its languid posture in the chair, 'I'm flattered that you were so touched by my absence that you strained to influence this return with such alacrity.'

'I feared that the longer you spent unbound the greater the chaos which would be inflicted upon the unwary public.'

With a shudder Kirkwood considered the implication of the blood he believed he had espied upon the creature's hands.

'Why do you care what becomes of them?'

The creature folded its hands in its lap and spoke with contempt in its voice.

'They are nothing to you. You are a selfish man, Kirkwood. Such I have learned about you during our acquaintance.'

'They are living, *human* beings,' Kirkwood said.

'Whilst I am neither?'

'Precisely.'

'And yet it was not the company of one of them which you craved in the night.' A sinister chuckle. 'Not even the one you married.'

Kirkwood bristled at mention of his matrimonial status. Grace Fanthorpe had been the choice of his parents as a match, and Richard found little fight within him to refuse the union, though it soon became apparent that his heart was not in it. They made a show of it for appearances' sake, even producing a son to carry on the family name, and they became firm friends, though little more. He concentrated his time and mind to his studies and she... did whatever women did with themselves in society. He felt sure she was relatively happy. Probably.

'Take a care with your words, demon, lest I limit your freedom yet further.'

He thrust back his shoulders and took a pace or two nearer to his captive.

'How would it feel if you were to be harnessed to that chair with manacles of iron at wrist and ankle?'

'Step closer still, my friend,' the demon tempted, 'and look into my eyes as you make your threats.'

Kirkwood felt his resolve melting under that gaze and turned swiftly away.

'You will not beguile me, demon.'

'I did before.'

Kirkwood shivered and slumped back into his chair at the desk.

'I was weak, led by my perverse desires.'

'There are no perversions,' the creature said,

'only limited minds. You showed no reticence then.'

'You took advantage of me.'

'And with those words you absolve yourself of any culpability,' it laughed. 'How convenient.'

'I will not be mocked by a thing dredged up from the depths of hell!'

The creature leapt to its feet and fire and fury swirled around it.

'And I will not be jeered at by a worm beneath my heel!'

In time the smoke drifted to the ceiling and dissipated as if it had never been, and Kirkwood's nerve returned.

'Yet the worm holds the key to your shackles, demon, you would do well to consider that.'

'I consider little else,' it replied, and the edge in its tone told of its subdued rage.

Kirkwood blanched, then set his jaw, affecting a confident demeanour.

'So, *my friend*,' he said, 'will you still refuse to tell me your name?'

The demon retook its seat and smiled a cruel smile.

'Names have power, Kirkwood, you know that.'

'You are already in my power,' Kirkwood said through gritted teeth.

'You called me here, you enchanted this circle,' the creature conceded. 'There lies the limit of your power over me.'

'With your name I could complete the spell to send you back to your own dark realm.'

'Perhaps.'

The smile widened.

'And so I will not tell it. And you cannot guess it.'

'No?'

'My name is beyond the comprehension of mortal men. It is many names in one. It means master and it means slave. I am called the fist as huge as mountains and the butterfly on the leaf. I am the Great One from the Blackness. Everything and anything and nothing in existence.'

'All that in a name?' Kirkwood's brow raised in incredulity.

'Why not keep it simple?' the thing suggested, with evident disdain. 'You can call me Jack.'

'Jack?'

'A common name hereabouts,' Jack shrugged. 'Easy to recall, easy to pronounce.'

'And quite harmless to you in terms of conjuration?'

Jack considered this with a stroke of its bearded chin.

'Frequent usage might afford it some little influence upon me.'

Kirkwood's interest was piqued. 'Oh?'

'Over a period of a hundred years or more,' Jack added, with a chuckle. 'But please, insert it into your incantations, let us see if it might repel me, eject me from this plane.'

'And risk freeing you onto the streets once more?' Kirkwood asked. 'I hardly think so.'

Jack shuffled in the chair, adjusting the cushions to its frame.

'Then I suppose I had better make myself comfortable,' it said. 'I could be here for a very long time.'

Chapter Four

Jack stood back and considered its artwork. Barely a portion of the thing lying so untidily before it was in its original position. The limbs were splayed awkwardly, the organs removed and scattered here and there. Jack had even taken parts of the features from the face and large hunks of flesh from the limbs and placed them on various surfaces around the room.

Having an enclosed space to pursue its hobby had pleased Jack immensely. The pretty, young blonde, who so willingly and unwittingly led the creature here, to this cramped room down a dark and dismal alleyway, would now be unrecognisable to her own mother, had such a figure been present to witness the scene. How pleasant to meet one so young and relatively fresh, compared to the worn, haggard things that usually called out and offered passing gentlemen *business* for a bargain price. Though undoubtedly tarnished by years of debasement, and not of the class of that first sweet slice of life from so many months earlier, this one was half the age of most of them, and her parts still tender and juicy.

Jack fondly recalled that first foray into the streets, after Kirkwood had carelessly mistaken his enchantments and freed the thing to sate its lusts. So many weak and feeble creatures swarming around, like insects to be swatted or squashed beneath the heel of the boots it had conjured, along with the swanky suit and spats, to more easily blend into its new surroundings.

A knife to strike with, so subtle, so quaint! Rending and slashing with talon and fang were the usual methods employed by the beast, yet subterfuge had seemed the wiser course, given the unfamiliar surroundings. Even with the furore surrounding Jack's later exploits, when Kirkwood's efforts to return Jack to its former home became ever more desperate and clumsy, releasing the demon ever more frequently as the year dwindled, that first victim had been overlooked and quickly forgotten. Against the butchery of those later killings the gentle execution of Clara Stobbs had been erroneously taken for the work of a mere human. In fact, her luckless spouse had been assumed at fault, supposedly enraged to discover that his wife had taken to the streets for money. Despite his denials the man had dangled from a rope scant months after Jack's first taste of human blood.

Though the constabulary and the press had yet to make a supernatural connection, they no longer attributed Jack's handiwork to domestic violence or other trivial happenstance. When Kirkwood related the stories presented by the most sensationalist of the newspapers, after each subsequent retrieval of his captive, it was with growing horror and desolation. He had quickly presumed that Jack was the perpetrator of the heinous crimes. The timings were beyond coincidence, and Jack made no secret of it after that first time. In his guilt at having initially tempted the creature into his home, his attempts to expel Jack from the mortal plane continued, leading to its freedom once more.

The meagre single room to which it had been led during the early hours, with the sparse furnishings and rank odour, at least provided shelter and privacy to allow the *artist* time to spend arranging the parts such as amused its devilish humour. No rushed and blundering hacking as out on the streets on those previous occasions. No, this time the act was cherished. A masterpiece!

One severed breast as pillow beneath the woman's head, the other by the feet. Intestines displayed on the right of the body, spleen to the left. The heart, moist and succulent, Jack had consumed whilst it was still warm.

As it admired its handiwork a breeze passed lightly through the broken pane in the window and caught the ragged curtain hanging there, lifting it slightly so that a shaft of daylight could dance across the tableau he had so adoringly created.

Daylight, the thing pondered. Had it lingered so long over its activities that night had crept silently away? Time then to retreat from this exercise and find sanctuary until the inevitable moment that Kirkwood should snatch it back into captivity within that cursed iron circle.

Jack looked down at its hands, its garments, the blade it clutched so affectionately. With its ability to fascinate and deceive the eyes of the humans that it might pass amongst, Jack had no fear of being perceived as drenched in the blood of its victim. Mortal eyes would detect only an average man of average appearance, in average garb, going about his average employ. But it would be best to be far from this scene before mortal eyes were able to fall upon its immortal frame.

As Jack turned towards the door a heavy fist pounded on the opposite side of it.

'Mary!' a male voice called. 'Are you in there?'

The knocking was hastily repeated. The handle rattled. It was fortunate that Jack's hostess had locked the door after they entered. Fortunate for Jack, if not for her.

'Come on, Mary. It's me, Tommy.'

Mary? Jack's erstwhile companion had claimed the name *Marie*. Perhaps the use of the more exotic, French-sounding name had suited her purposes, lifted her esteem in the eyes of her clientele? It mattered little now.

'Mary?' Tommy persisted. 'If you're there you'll 'ave to open up. McCarthy's sent me. Your back rent is up to thirty bob, now, and 'e's not 'avin' it.'

Another single bang, lower down. In his frustration Tommy had launched a kick at the barrier keeping him out.

Jack became aware of the scuffing of boots on the ground beyond the door. Had Tommy concluded that she whom he sought was not within and decided to leave? Then there came the silhouette of a young human male on the curtain at the window, and a hand reaching through the broken pane and tugging at the tatty material. Jack barely had time to step back into the shadows, out of view, before the cry of horror echoed through the courtyard outside.

Any plans to quickly retreat from the area before the visitor returned were dashed when Jack peeped from the door and saw the man duck into a shop entrance at the end of the passageway. Raised voices could be heard and a moment later the shop doorway opened once again to allow egress to the same man and an older, heavier man, who was dragging on his jacket and grumbling audibly.

'Thomas Bowyer, if you're 'aving me on...!'

'I wouldn't, Mr McCarthy,' Tommy gasped. 'Not over somethin' like this.'

Jack hastily re-secured the door to the tiny apartment and took its place in the corner. The curtain moved; daylight illuminated the grisly spectacle within the room.

'Christ on a bicycle!' McCarthy swore. 'God spare my poor eyes!'

He stepped away and the curtain dropped back into place.

'Tommy,' McCarthy urged, 'get off down to the Commercial Street station, get the coppers here, sharpish!'

Only one set of footsteps clattered down the alley. McCarthy remained on guard outside. Jack weighed the option of tearing McCarthy asunder and making a run for it against waiting out the return of the other man. But his only means of escape would be by the same passageway through which a stampede of police constables would be tramping at any moment. However innocent he might make himself appear to their eyes, his very presence in this location would be suspicious enough to cause them to detain the creature. Or attempt to.

Very soon heavy boots and heavier voices told of Tommy's arrival, amongst a large contingent of law enforcement officials.

'I'm Inspector Beck,' a new voice announced. 'Is this the window? Step aside now, let me see.'

The curtain twitched, followed by a sharp intake of breath.

'Lord preserve us!' Beck spluttered.

He cleared his throat and his voice was strong once more.

'You men, seal off the streets nearby. No one in or out except on my say so. Get the police surgeon down here right now. And send for Inspector Abberline.'

To one who has endured untold eons in a realm beyond human understanding, time makes little impression. Minutes, hours, days, all are as one. Jack stood in the shadows of that blood-splattered room as more humans arrived, and more eyes peered through the window. Someone suggested waiting for the arrival of bloodhounds before forcing entry. Neighbouring doors were hammered upon, residents roused and questioned. A camera was thrust though the window, its flash throwing harsh radiance over the devastated corpse.

After hours had passed, yet another new voice announced that the bloodhounds were not available after all.

'Get that blasted door open!' Beck yelled.

'I've got a pick-axe indoors,' McCarthy said, and within moments the first crashing strike was made against the lock.

Jack bared its fangs and growled.

Chapter Five

'"*The sight we saw I cannot drive away from my mind*, said John McCarthy, landlord of 13 Miller's Court, the scene of the atrocity. *It looked more like the work of a devil than of a man.*"'

Kirkwood hurled the newspaper into the fire, where flames swiftly consumed it.

'A devil!'

'How astute. Our Mr McCarthy seemed a splendid fellow. I was looking forward to making his acquaintance,' said Jack, back in place in its usual chair. 'Your timely intervention spoiled what might have been an interesting, if rather brief, relationship.'

'Had I been aware of that then I might have delayed,' Kirkwood said. 'Allowed them time to clap you in iron cuffs, and trap you behind iron bars.'

'A noble sentiment, I'm sure,' returned Jack, 'though we both know that that would not have been the outcome of such a conflict. Before any restraints could be applied I would have shredded their ranks like a scythe through a field of corn.'

'They suspect your nature,' Kirkwood snarled. 'You go too far!'

'I go as far as my whim takes me, Kirkwood,' Jack replied. 'Were I fully at liberty then this city would be bowing down to me, if not this whole world.'

'That is why you may never be free,' Kirkwood said. 'I'll find a way to expel you from this place, and be gladly rid of you.'

'Such harsh words,' Jack said. 'And I thought we were becoming good friends.'

'Never that!' Kirkwood said.

'You forget our first encounter,' Jack said, voice oozing poisoned honey. 'The warm tenderness in that preliminary greeting.'

'That was a mistake.'

'One you relished at the time.'

'Which merely shows what a fool I was.'

Jack sat back, and spread its hands in a gesture of helplessness.

'I am your creature, Richard Kirkwood. Your plaything, to do with as you will.'

Kirkwood rested his elbows on his desk, drooping his head onto his forearms.

'You play the compliant servant well, when it suits your purposes.'

'You look tired, Kirkwood.'

Kirkwood could not find the strength even to lift his head and cast a scornful look at his captive.

'Do you wonder?'

'Why continue in this fruitless pursuit? Come over here, kick away these chains, put an end to your exhausting efforts.'

'And close my eyes to what happens next?'

'If it helps you sleep.'

'You can return yourself whence you came at any time it pleases you,' Kirkwood said. 'Why would you allow this confinement, this indignity, to persist, when you could just go home?'

'Why would I?'

Jack breathed in deeply though its nose, as if drawing in the scents of the world around it.

'There are such rich pleasures to be savoured on those darkened streets.'

'You want an end to this,' Kirkwood pleaded.

'So end it.'

'My patience has no limit, mortal. You will break before I do.'

Kirkwood peeled himself from his seat, went to a small cabinet against the wall. He took out a decanter of brandy and a glass, pouring himself a generous measure.

'Brandy, Kirkwood?' said Jack. 'Are you feeling the chill?'

'Whenever I'm in your company.'

Jack's lips curled into some semblance of a smile.

'Your wit improves. Could it be I'm having an influence upon you?'

'Let us pray not.'

Kirkwood drained the glass and refilled it.

Jack leaned forward, elbows on knees, keen eyes burning into its host.

'The responsibility for my activities whilst abroad in this world falls entirely on your shoulders.'

Kirkwood returned to his seat, those shoulders heavy with the truth of Jack's words.

'But why so down-hearted?' Jack continued. 'There is no blood upon your doorstep.'

Kirkwood raised his gaze, but quickly averted his eyes from the mesmeric stare of the demon.

'The residents of those grim streets have as much right to live as anyone here in these mean quarters of the city.'

Jack chuckled maliciously.

'You don't entirely believe that.'

'They're still human beings, for God's sake!'

'Just barely.'

Jack sat back and crossed its long legs, arrogant posture displaying the depth of its contempt.

'Do not pretend with me. Your disgust is for the indiscretion of my actions, not my choice of whomsoever I may "act" upon.'

'You make presumptions, demon!'

Kirkwood stood, weighing the glass in his hand, tempted to hurl it at the being facing him. Instead he returned to the drink cabinet and refilled it.

'Do not let your soul become so troubled just yet, Kirkwood. Leave me some room for play, once you give it to me.'

In his anger Kirkwood stepped closer to the circle of chains, lips parted to spill forth some profanity or other, but he regained himself, teeth gritted, and resumed his seat.

'It is not yours to toy with, creature,' he said, barely a quiver in his voice. 'I have not promised it.'

'And nor need you.'

Long fingers gestured towards the encircling chains.

'Remove the iron. Set me free. There is many a desperate rogue out there who would gladly bargain away eternity on a fancy.'

'You shall not tread beyond these walls again,' Kirkwood swore.

He downed his drink, and imagined the tear in his eye was prompted by the harsh bite of the liquor.

Silence held sway over the room, broken by the cries of street hawkers and pedlars plying their trades on the rough pavements two floors below.

Jack tapped thick, curved fingernails on the arms of its chair.

'You could come with me,' it said, voice soft, coaxing.

Kirkwood stared, incredulous.

'What?!'

'Think of it. The power! At my side you could strut those moon-drenched streets like a king; untouchable, unstoppable.'

'And do what? Destroy more misbegotten, gutter-crawling wretches. Hack their flesh? Swim in their blood? Taste their organs like they were some delicacy from a far-off land?'

Jack licked its lips.

'How sweet they are! And tender! Especially as you watch the fear in their eyes fade to nothing, and hear their screams drowned by their own blood. It's intoxicating, Kirkwood!'

Kirkwood stood and covered his ears with his hands.

'Silence! I will hear no more of this horror.'

'The thought excites you,' Jack said, harsh voice penetrating Kirkwood's defences. 'I can hear your pulse racing.'

'It is revulsion that sets my heart pounding, monster!'

Kirkwood pointed a shaking finger at the beast.

'You cannot entice me to join you in your carnage.'

'You tell me what you yourself want to hear,' Jack laughed, 'but I see beyond your bluster.'

Kirkwood collapsed back into his chair. 'It's not true,' he whimpered. 'You're lying.'

But as those words sank into his brain, and he felt the hammering in his chest, the flushing in his face, the raising of the fine hairs on his neck and forearms, he wondered if there could be some measure of veracity in what the demon said. He closed his eyes and saw the gushing of another's blood on his hands. He felt the blade he held plunge into another's flesh, and he thrust again, savouring the sensation as the organs spilled free.

Had corruption claimed him, after prolonged proximity to the hell-spawned thing before him? Or had there always been a part of him that yearned for dominion over a lesser, weaker being than himself? Whichever was the case, he knew that he was lost.

'To think that I was so deluded as to believe that one such as you could be the answer to my prayers.'

'You know I will grant any wish you have,' Jack teased.

'But your price is too high.'

Kirkwood strode towards the circle, toes almost touching the chains.

'Damn you, demon! I cannot force you to return to your hellish province,' he said, 'but likewise I cannot break your confinement and free you once more into the world.'

Jack stood, towering over the human, boots inches from Kirkwood's.

'Then the stalemate prevails. This accursed circle shall remain my prison until this house crumbles around me. Or until your resolve weakens and you unleash me.'

'A third option occurs to me,' Kirkwood said, a haunted expression on his face.

'A third?'

Jack's brow furrowed in a deep frown.

'You can only mean—'

Before Jack could finish, Kirkwood steeled his nerve and stepped past Jack, inside the chain circle.

'Fool!' Jack bellowed. 'The magicks which confine me will now bind you also.'

It reared up, fangs and talons bared.

'I know this,' Kirkwood said. 'And I know you cannot do your summoner physical harm, so I do not fear your claws.'

'So what now?' Jack said. 'Do you intend to wither and die in here alongside me, content in the knowledge that I cannot be released?'

'No, for you have already proclaimed your infinite patience. Once I am dust someone would come along and remove the iron, unaware of the horror they would be letting loose.'

'Then what is your plan?'

Plan? Kirkwood reflected. Could this manic notion be dignified with such a description? All options considered and dismissed, this had been the only remaining route left to him.

'I accept your bargain, demon. My soul for my heart's desire.'

'And what is it that your feeble heart craves, Kirkwood?'

'That you be banished from this plane.'

He closed his eyes, so that the creature would not see the fear in them.

'My folly brought you here, and my ineptitude allowed you to remain. Let my living essence complete the spell to return you to your netherworld.'

'You would really give your life to send me home?'

'I would.'

Jack's face twisted into a shape which could have been a snarl or a smile. It placed its hands on Kirkwood's shoulders.

'So be it. You forfeit yourself to sate my lusts. But don't expect anyone, above or below, to have mercy on your soul.'

The demon's final words had echoed like the

entire hordes of Hades screeching as one. The flames of a thousand fires burst into life in that small ring of iron, consuming all within, drowning the screams of the human soul writhing in absolute and ultimate agony.

By the time the fires had faded all that remained inside the chain circle was dust.

Book Two

Thomas Kirkwood

Chapter Six

The black cab pulled up at the kerb. The passenger leaned forward to pass the fare through the sliding screen then clambered from the vehicle. He watched the cab pull away along the empty, litter-strewn street, disappearing around a corner where a boarded-up shop sat gloomy and forlorn, despite the autumn sunshine glaring down on it and the bright colours of the graffiti adorning its frontage. The narrow lane separating this street from the next was like a portal between different worlds, different times. Forgotten back roads such as this were rare in an area like Tower Hamlets, a relatively new borough, formed in 1965 and covering much of London's East End, and they clung feebly to their identity amid the new developments creeping closer from all sides. Already the cab would be slowing as it merged into the busy traffic at the next corner, swerving between bright red double-decker buses, workmen's vans, cars and taxis to be quickly swallowed up in the flow. In the distance shiny new tower blocks dwarfed the dark, portico-lined terrace behind the new arrival, peering down on the crumbling buildings, like a healthy youth sneering at the elderly man tottering along on his walking stick.

Thomas Kirkwood regarded the tall portal, with its high arched recess and heavy door, paintwork chipped and peeling, and the dull, brown bricked walls, weather-worn and stained, and a private smile twitched his lips. It may be anachronistic and dilapidated but there was something about the old place that appealed to him.

He fished the chunky, iron key from the pocket of his jacket and approached the door. His door. The door of the house he didn't even know he owned until a few days ago.

The small firm of solicitors which had served his family for generations had closed down when the elderly head of the company had succumbed to the COVID-19 virus. The remaining board members had wound up the business and fled to more highly-regarded positions in larger companies in the City. The new firm that Thomas had hired to take over the Kirkwood portfolio had requested an interview in which they would discuss the entire range of investments and properties, so as to be fully transparent at the beginning of their relationship. Also, as Thomas had passed the age of fifty, they felt he should have a new will made out, comprehensively listing the disbursements of his estate in fine detail.

The deeds to this building, which stood long disused and uninhabited, lay hidden amongst the faded documents deep in the vaults of the defunct company. Retrieved, dust blown off, they were presented to Thomas at the consultation and caused much interest and amused discussion. A property of this size and in this location, shown a little care and attention, would be worth a considerable amount on the housing market. That it had lain untouched for so long was inconceivable to a roomful of opportunist businessmen.

But it came with a mystery.

Bought by one of Thomas's ancestors over 130 years ago as a second home where he could study and carry out unspecified experimentation in privacy and solitude, this earlier Mr Kirkwood had apparently abandoned the house and disappeared without informing his wife or family.

Intrigued by the story Thomas declined his new solicitor's offer to find a buyer for the house, deciding instead to investigate the mystery for his own personal satisfaction.

The last visitor to the property had been Thomas's own father, Eric, in 1979. The paperwork showed that a brief survey had been made, certain renovations carried out and an inventory made of the contents and fittings. Some items of furnishing were listed which had been removed or replaced: a desk chair, moth-eaten and riddled with woodworm, a grandfather clock, its mechanism seized and irreparable. Parts of this inventory had later been redacted and pages removed, and there was a note bearing Eric Kirkwood's signature ordering that the building be secured and left undisturbed until further notice. No further notice was forthcoming and over time the place was neglected and forgotten.

Thomas had taken the file and the key away with him, intent on visiting the house as soon as an opportunity arose. His wife, Emma, had shown little interest in his tales of mysterious disappearances from so long ago, and his son, Luke, almost 21 years old, was more concerned with spending the family fortune than discovering more about where it came from. Plenty of time to educate him once he had burned off some of his youthful energy.

And so Thomas had made the journey here

alone.

The metalwork forged into the door seemed too old to have been part of his father's security measures, perhaps dating back to the time of his antecedent, the first Kirkwood to own the place. Bars at the windows protected iron shutters. He wasn't surprised to discover scratches and gouges around the lock and over the sunken hinges, suggesting that attempts had been made to break into the house over the intervening years, if unsuccessfully. Thomas reflected that little short of an atomic bomb would penetrate these defences. He patted the door and felt no vibration, heard no rattle of loose fittings. It was like slapping a hand against solid rock. After a moment's pressure the key made a gratifying clunking sound as it turned the mechanism within the lock, and the creaking groan as the door swung open would have suited a black and white horror movie.

The gothic horror impression continued as Thomas stepped inside, a chill in stark contrast to the warm afternoon outside sweeping past him, as if seeking escape after its long imprisonment. Power had been restored so a flick of a switch dispelled the darkness in the hallway, though a sense of gloom remained, heavy and foreboding, which a forty-odd year old lightbulb could not dissipate.

The rooms on the ground floor were empty of all but dust and cobwebs, confirming the remaining listings on the inventory, which suggested that the lower floor had never been used and any activity was confined to the upper level. The narrow staircase rose steeply, and was soon swallowed in shadow. Thomas looked for a second light switch, hoping to illuminate the upper hallway before ascending, but he couldn't find one. He assumed it must be at the top of the stairs, so he cautiously ventured upwards, testing each tread before putting his full weight on it. One hand held the bannister rail, the other swept up the wall, steadying him and seeking out the elusive switch. An L-shape struck off to the right from a small landing three steps from the top and the feeble amount of light filtering from below was lost. The darkness was a solid wall ahead of him, an ominous presence stealing his vision away. Thomas saw himself watching this scene in a scratchy old movie on TV, calling out at the set, 'Don't go up there! Why would you go up there?' His usually stoic and phlegmatic mind created various gruesome creatures to inhabit the stygian depths of the unseen corridor. But this was no film, just an old house with poor lighting, despite the eerie atmosphere permeating the place. With a shudder, Thomas took his mobile phone from his pocket and called up the torch app. Shadows danced and frolicked around the swaying light, like ghostly children at play. The beam revealed the switch, just within reach. He gratefully thumbed the rocker and abruptly the hallway was just a hallway.

A bedroom, modestly equipped, a bathroom, similarly spartan, and another empty room were the first chambers Thomas discovered on the upper floor. The remaining door, standing firmly closed at the far end of the hall, must belong to the study mentioned in the survey, where his ancestor had carried out his mysterious research.

The house as a whole had a fusty odour, Thomas felt his nose and throat becoming more dry and clogged every moment he spent here, but upon opening the study door he detected another smell, something rank, lurking in the room. Had some unfortunate creature found its way in here, become trapped and died? How could that happen? The building had withstood the assaults of thieves and vandals, nothing bigger than a flea could penetrate these walls. His questions went unanswered, as no carcass lay curled in the corner of the room or hidden behind the few items of furniture, and soon the smell dissipated and was forgotten.

A small, shabby chaise longue, a bookcase, and a drinks cabinet were overpowered by the large desk which dominated the space. By the marble fireplace, where a chair might be expected to be found close to the tiled hearth, Thomas detected a curious mark on the floorboards, as if they had been scorched at one time and some attempt had been made to eradicate the traces.

Prominently displayed on numerous shelves and surfaces were several grotesque statues of hideous, devilish figures, and skulls which appeared to be genuine human remains. His father's inventory had glossed over these abhorrent items, listing them as 'peculiar decorative artefacts'.

Thomas shuddered and continued his survey.

Overhead an elaborate chandelier bore evidence of its passage into the present day. An electric cord was visible coiling around the suspending chain and glass bulbs resided where once candles would have been fitted.

The swivel chair which stood by the desk was clearly of a design introduced in the 1970s, with gas riser and moulded backrest, and would undoubtedly have been brought in by his father during his renovating process. Brushing the dust from the cushioned seat Thomas sat at the desk, hands resting on the leather inset, and tried to sense the thoughts which occupied the mind of Richard Kirkwood all those years ago.

Some impulse, almost like a faint voice whispering close to his ear, made him reach out and slide open the top drawer. Reaching inside he removed the ancient, ornately-bound book and placed it before him, lifting the cover and turning the stiff, delicate pages.

Chapter Seven

High walls and thick hedges lined the narrow road, shielding the sprawling properties beyond from prying eyes. The moon sat high in the clear sky, glinting off the silver paintwork of the big, flashy car purring its way along the winding route. Soon it reached a large, pillared entrance. Massive iron gates responded to the signal from within the car and swung aside to allow it through.

About an hour's drive from London, via the M3, this was one of the most exclusive areas in England, within the administrative county of Guildford, Surrey. On this elite estate north of the town, nestled in its extensive, well-maintained gardens, sat a Georgian style villa, featuring five bedroom suites, with additional staff quarters, two large kitchens and an impressive leisure and entertainment complex.

Thomas Kirkwood drove his Bentley Continental along the drive of the grand house and around to the rear, headlights flashing off the windows of the indoor pool area. Condensation dripped down the thick glass doors as he pushed his way through them and passed the steam room and sauna to reach the 15m egg-shaped pool. He knew that at this time of the evening the most likely place to find his wife would be lounging poolside with a gin and a lurid novel.

'Hello, darling,' he said, leaning in and placing a gentle peck on the top of her head.

She tilted her head back so that he could

repeat the kiss on her lips. He slipped a hand inside her robe as the moment lingered.

'You're late,' she grumbled, playfully. 'I was beginning to think you'd forgotten me.'

'As if I ever could.'

He lifted her empty glass from the table at her side and crossed to the chilled drinks cabinet by the wall.

'Refill?'

'Mmm, thanks.'

'G and T?'

'Of course.'

He poured her drink, and a whisky for himself, and brought them over, slipping off his jacket and slumping onto the lounger next to hers.

'Tired?' she asked.

He grunted in confirmation, feeling the weight of his aching muscles easing as he lay there, the fatigue slowly draining from him, leaching into the cushions beneath his back.

'Why don't we take these upstairs?' she suggested. 'Have an early night?'

She smiled and put her hand on his. He frowned, eyes on the glass-panelled ceiling.

She leaned closer.

'What's the matter?'

He shook his head, shrugged.

'It's nothing.'

'You look troubled.'

'No.'

He tried a smile, but failed.

She pulled off his tie, loosened a couple of shirt buttons.

'Is it the business?' she teased. 'Are we ruined? Will we have to sell up? Leave all this behind? Go and live in a yurt?'

'Sounds idyllic,' he laughed. 'No, we're secure.'

'Then what?'

'I wanted to have another look at those books tonight,' he said.

He didn't have to specify which books he meant. He had been spending every spare moment lately studying the scratchy writing in the notebooks he had found in that desk in the old house in the City. They had been crammed in the drawer along with the big book. The spooky book. The one that gave you the shivers if you read it for too long. Evidently his ancestor had been trying to decipher the secrets of the old tome, and some of his findings were startling, to say the least.

But not that book. Not tonight. It wasn't here at home. He didn't want it here, and he couldn't bring himself to remove it from the old house. Though sometimes he imagined it was more that the book itself didn't want to leave.

'Oh, not tonight, darling, please. You're dead on your feet.'

'Just a few minutes. There's something I want to go over.'

'What on earth is in those dusty, crumbly old ledgers that fascinates you so much?'

He sat up, sipped his drink, rubbed his eyes.

'It's not easy to say.'

'Whatever it is,' she coaxed, 'you can talk to me.'

'I know.'

Communication had never been an issue between them. During almost twenty-five years of marriage, bringing up a bright and boisterous son, enjoying a healthy and happy life, they had never kept anything from one another.

He'd been barely older than Luke is now when

they met. Brash, confident, snugly nestled under his father's wing, learning the family business with the vast safety net of being the boss's son. She was the daughter of a politician who was firmly ensconced in a comfortable Tory seat, made all the more comfortable by family money and his inflated salary.

But an open and frank relationship wasn't the issue. This was far beyond the measure of his limited understanding to adequately explain.

'I've been spending a lot of time lately... contemplating my death,' he began, falteringly.

He raised a hand to forestall he interruption he anticipated.

'And yours. And Luke's.'

'But why?'

He ignored her, pressed on.

'And the demise of every person who lives, and who ever has lived.'

She sat back, watched him, concern creasing her pretty face.

'Death is a fact of life.' He smiled grimly. 'It's a cliché because it's true. "It comes to us all." We're all aware of it, yet we know so little about it. It's a symptom of the human condition that, given the brevity of life, we obsess about death.'

'I can't say I spend too much time consumed with the notion,' she said lightly, sipping her drink.

'Life is short and then... what's next?'

'Next?'

'Is this it? Is there no more to human existence than floating through space on this desolate rock, scrambling around for a short time in these worthless sacks of flesh and bone?'

She unfastened her robe, allowed it to fall away from her slender frame, scarcely concealed in the skimpy swimsuit.

'Speak for yourself, darling.'

He allowed his eyes to roam the length of her.

'All right, point taken,' he said, through his toothy grin. 'But you know what I mean. Do we just have this blink of life then, puff...!'

He spread his empty hands.

'Snuffed out like a candle, without so much as a wisp of smoke left behind?'

He stood, stretched, returned to the drinks cabinet.

'Or is there more to us than the mere corporeal shell we travel around in? Spirit? Soul, perhaps? And can that part exist beyond the corruption of the flesh? If so, where does it go once the vessel it travelled around in is no more? Does it stay among us? Are we, even now, surrounded by the ghosts of billions of people who passed before us?'

Emma refastened her robe with a shudder.

'Urgh! What a depressing thought.'

'Exactly.'

Thomas raised his glass to tight lips.

'Almost as depressing as the idea that we have this single life and nothing more. So, we have to ponder the question of other worlds, other planes of existence. Places where, once our bodies have failed us, we can travel to and continue to exist.'

'Heaven?' Emma suggested.

Thomas scoffed and knocked back his whisky.

'I sincerely doubt it.'

'Some form of life after death, then?'

'Exactly.'

He lifted the gin bottle, waggled it in his fingers. Emma shook her head. He poured another whisky and returned to his seat.

'So if our consciousness goes on, and eventually finds its way to some sort of "eternal beyond", could it someday, somehow, find its way back?'

'Come back?'

She gaped at him.

'Return from this "beyond"?'

'In some form.'

'Like reincarnation?'

He shrugged.

'Most theories of reincarnation suggest that the consciousness is lost.' He chuckled. 'Rebooted, to coin a contemporary phrase. Leaving behind its memories, the awareness of its former life, in the process of rebirth.'

'So what are you asking?'

Emma sat up, tugged her robe tighter around herself. Goosebumps were prickling her arms, as if there was a chill in the room. She glanced towards the door, so see if Thomas had left it open when he entered, but it was firmly closed.

'Is there a way to come back as you were before?'

Thomas smiled, grimly.

'There's no point in coming back to a body that's let you down once already. That'll be under the ground, anyway. Or in an urn on your mantelpiece. But the mind, at least, and the memories of who you were, somehow renewed.'

She held out her glass to him.

'I will have another, after all.'

'I'm sorry, darling,' he said, taking the glass. 'I didn't mean to weigh you down with existential angst on a balmy evening.'

'Are you ill? Is that what's brought on all this maudlin talk?'

'No, nothing like that.'

He laughed, handing back the refreshed drink.

'There's a few years left in this old shell yet, I hope.'

She stood, moved to him, wrapped her arms around him.

'A mid-life crisis, then?'

She touched his face.

'I think I'd prefer it if you'd spent all our savings on a motor cycle and a canal boat.'

He laughed, and kissed her forehead.

'Come to bed,' she said. 'Leave those horrible books for tonight.'

'Okay.'

He nodded, squeezed her in his embrace, kissed her lips.

'I think I'll go up to the city for the weekend, take all this doom and gloom out of your way.'

'There's no need.'

'I know, but it'll be easier there, I'll have all the notes in one place.'

'That horrid little place of yours.'

He felt her shaking in his arms.

'It serves a purpose,' he said.

'I'm not sure what.'

She appraised him with eyebrows raised.

'Why you didn't just get rid of it last year when you first learned it existed is beyond me.'

'There's something about the place.'

He frowned, his mind grasping at elusive notions.

'Some attraction, some compulsion that keeps calling me back.'

'Really?' she said, eyebrow arched sardonically. 'Attractive, it is not.'

She finished her drink, put the glass on the table.

'Come on, death will keep for another night.'

He smiled and took her hand, following her through the door into the interior of the house, but her last words lingered in his head, and a brief shiver ran through him.

Chapter Eight

Thomas Kirkwood had allowed himself to become so deeply engrossed in the notebooks spread across the old desk that the ding-dong sound from his mobile phone startled him from an almost trancelike state. An image appeared on the screen, a face distorted by its proximity to the camera at the front door as the caller leaned forward to press the buzzer again. Thomas had arranged for the video intercom system to be installed because, with such a robust door and the study situated at the opposite end of the house, a visitor might pound their knuckles to dust before being heard.

That was one of a number of improvements he had initiated since taking over the place the year before. The bedrooms were now furnished, in case Emma and Luke ever decided that they wanted to spend time here, the electrics had been updated, and the building had been thoroughly cleaned. Curiously, the agency appointed to maintain the house had changed the regular cleaner three times already, as they always complained that the place was 'too creepy' for them. Though he had been here a number of times since his first visit Thomas too had never quite shaken off that earliest impression of a cold, forbidding vault of dark secrets, despite the weird fascination that continually drew him back here. To this house. To this study. To these books.

Thomas checked his Rolex. His guest was suitably punctual, a trait Thomas strongly valued. He pressed a button on the phone screen, opening communication with the speaker at the door.

'Mr Phillips?'

The man looked round, puzzled by the disembodied voice.

'Indeed,' he said. 'That is I.'

He frowned, corrected himself.

'Me.'

Reconsidered.

'I am he.'

Thomas sighed. Was this the 'expert' who had been recommended to him? As he strode the long corridor and trotted down the stairs he reminded himself not to make snap judgements. The 'finder', to whom he had delegated the task of locating a person with the precise set of talents he required, had spoken highly of this man's knowledge and reputation.

'Do come in, Mr Phillips,' Thomas said, swinging open the heavy door.

With a nervous smile and nod the little man shuffled into the hallway. In his old-fashioned tweeds and with his round, open face, it was difficult for Thomas to guess his age. He fussed and bowed with the mannerisms of an old professor, enhanced with the energy of a much younger man.

'Please, call me H.P.' he said, pushing his round-rimmed spectacles up his nose.

'I won't, if you don't mind,' said Thomas, leading the way up the stairs. 'That's a little informal. I don't think we're there yet.'

'Oh, sorry.'

Howard Phillips scuttled after him, hurrying to make up the distance gained by Thomas's longer legs.

Once Howard had caught him up Thomas waved a hand towards the *chaise*, watching with some distaste as he perched on the edge of the seat, as if expecting to be reprimanded for some unknown offence.

'Relax,' Thomas said.

Howard hitched himself further onto the cushion, though appeared no less tense.

Thomas settled into the large Chesterfield armchair he'd had placed in the spot where he imagined a similar chair once stood, many years earlier. As he gripped the arms he felt the now-familiar shiver up his spine, a stirring within him, not from a chill, but rather from a sense of elation, of empowerment. He took a moment to savour the sensation before speaking.

'I expect you're wondering why I wanted to talk to you.'

'I have an inkling,' his guest said.

Thomas smiled at the choice of phrase.

'Have you, indeed?'

He paused, waiting, forcing the nervy man to explain his words.

'Well,' Howard began, 'this place has quite a reputation amongst the aware.'

'It does, does it?'

'Oh yes!' Howard said, missing the sardonic edge in Thomas's tone. 'Famous, you might say.'

'I hadn't a clue this place even existed until a year ago,' Thomas said, folding his hands in his lap. 'Yet you say it's famous?'

'Perhaps famous is a stretch,' Howard admitted. 'But certainly well-known, in certain circles.'

'Such as amongst "the aware"?'

'Indeed,' Howard said, patting his thighs in delight.

He gave Thomas an encouraging smile, like a teacher to a bright pupil. Thomas's instinct was to be affronted at being patronised, but Howard's puppy-like candour and enthusiasm made it impossible to take offence.

'And who are these "aware?"'

'Those of us who know about the mysteries which surround us.'

'Mysteries?'

'Unknown forces. Limitless energies.'

Howard's eyes grew wide as he spoke.

'Entities who constantly traverse between worlds.'

Thomas stared, unsure of how to respond.

'We're not alone,' Howard went on.

Thomas glanced around the room.

'I rather hope we are,' he said, attempting to keep the mood light.

Howard's response was deeply earnest.

'We're not.'

Thomas took a moment to process this.

'I was hoping,' he said, 'that your extensive studies into, er...'

He stopped. How the hell did he label what this man studied?

Howard provided the description for him.

'The arcane.'

'Quite.'

Thomas experienced an uneasy turning of the tables. This quiet, mousy man sat before him speaking of forces and energies and alien entities with such utter conviction that, instead of laughing or calling him insane, Thomas was a little awestruck.

He cleared his throat before resuming.

'That your studies would give you an insight into some strange occurrences which have taken place within these walls.'

Howard shuffled back to the edge of his seat, leaning in closer.

'Intriguing,' he said. 'Please, go on.'

Thomas took a breath as he formed his thoughts.

'This house has been in the possession of my family for many years,' he began. 'A little over one hundred and thirty years ago there was an... incident.'

'Please, Mr Kirkwood,' said Howard, taking a handkerchief from his pocket and polishing his glasses. 'If you continue to use these pretty euphemisms to trim your story we'll never reach the heart of the matter.'

Thomas accepted the gentle rebuke with a gracious smile.

'Fair enough, Mr Phillips. My ancestor, Richard Kirkwood, was resident here at the time, and he suddenly upped and disappeared without trace. To this day no one knows what happened to him.'

'I see.'

Howard replaced his glasses, nodding sagely.

'And what was it that made you seek out my assistance?'

With a wave of a hand Thomas indicated the skulls, candles and graven images which still adorned the shelves and walls.

'These items you see around the place...'

'Occult paraphernalia.'

Howard studied the pieces with a critical eye.

'I had noticed.'

'They belonged to him.'

'The afore-mentioned Richard Kirkwood?'

'Yes,' Thomas confirmed. 'He was heavily into studies of the arcane.'

'As am I,' Howard said, somewhat unnecessarily.

'As, indeed, are you.'

Thomas spread his hands, point made.

'I believe,' he continued, cupping his chin in one hand thoughtfully, 'that something he discovered may have been responsible for what happened to him.'

'Oh?'

Howard shuffled on the *chaise longue* again, head cocked, expression keen, giving Thomas the impression of a squirrel watching a housewife fill a bird-feeder.

'How so?'

'Your guess, I dare say, will be far better than mine.'

'Ah, I see,' said Howard, as if they had reached the only logical conclusion.

'You have quite a reputation, Mr Phillips.'

Howard blushed and shook his head.

'I have attempted to make sense of the extensive writings of my antecedent and, whilst quite fascinated, I am still also quite baffled. Your knowledge is undoubtedly far beyond my own.'

'Then perhaps I might be allowed...?'

Howard shuffled even further forward, his attitude ardent, his eyes imploring. Another inch, Thomas realised, and he would be crouching in mid-air. He decided to take pity on the funny little man.

'That was my purpose in inviting you here, Mr Phillips,' he said, rising and making his way to the large desk.

Howard eagerly stood and followed him.

'I may be ready to call you Howard,' Thomas said.

Howard beamed, delighted.

'H.P.'

'I don't do nicknames.'

'Oh,' Howard said, crestfallen.

'And I'm Thomas.'

'Ah!' The smile returned.

'Not Tom.'

'Of course.'

Thomas indicated the documents still lying on the desk.

'These are his notebooks.'

He pointed out a more modern notepad amongst the yellowed booklets.

'And my own interpretation of them.'

Howard picked up one of the books, flicked through the pages, exchanged it for another, repeated the procedure a number of times, occasionally referring back to one he had already examined, all the time oohing and aahing at significant passages.

Thomas stood by, hands in pockets, watching him patiently.

Then, gradually, less patiently.

'Any thoughts?' Thomas eventually asked.

Howard looked up from the pages, noticed Thomas's barely disguised scowl.

'Yes! Yes! My apologies, Mr Thomas.'

He lifted one of the books, patting the pages delicately and reverentially.

'The prior Kirkwood was heavily interested in the secret magic of the dark times, an era of civilisation that existed long before those we are taught of in the standard school curricula.'

Howard's eyes were unfocused, staring at objects and locations far beyond the walls around them. His voice softened, as if his words were for himself alone, and Thomas cocked his head to hear him better.

'Unimaginable powers were manipulated by the mystical practitioners of these long-gone days, strong enough to force the elements themselves to do their bidding. And to control the inhabitants of the alternative planes of existence they discovered through their learning and exploration.'

He blinked, back in the real world, and turned to Thomas, concern creasing his features.

'I hope I'm not losing you, Thomas?'

'I'm hanging on,' Thomas smiled. 'Just barely.'

Howard seemed not to notice Thomas's teasing.

'Good, good.'

He pointed out a note in Richard Kirkwood's scratchy handwriting.

'Now, this manuscript mentioned here...?'

'Oh yes,' said Thomas, turning to the desk and reaching into one of the drawers. 'That's probably this one.'

Thomas heard Howard's breath catch in his throat as he lifted the old book into view, and a tiny squeal of excitement as the small, dapper man tried to speak. Thomas held out the book and Howard's eyes almost popped out of his head at the prospect of actually touching it. He reached out a hesitant hand, not quite daring to take it.

The tableau persisted for long seconds, until Thomas thrust the book into Howard's shaky hands.

'Take it, take it!'

Howard finally did so, squealing again as he stroked the dusty leather. He opened the cover, eyes flitting over the faded text, sniffing the musky scent of the pages, and another small squeal escaped him.

Thomas gave him an indulgent smile.

'You're squeaking, Howard.'

Howard took a moment, regained his composure.

'Yes, yes, sorry. It's just, well...'

He held the book against his chest, hugged it like a lost child.

'This is the Magoralian Text.'

Thomas shrugged.

'Is it?'

'An ancient Book of Shadows.'

He lifted it closer to his face and Thomas wondered if he was going to kiss it.

'Also called the Book of Secret Names. The Chronicle of Calling. The Lost Words of Invocation.'

'One title wasn't enough for them?'

He looked at the book Howard clasped so tightly, wanting to be impressed but not quite getting it.

'I take it this is an important book, then?'

Howard looked at him, aghast.

'More than important, it's immensely powerful!'

Thomas opened his mouth to speak, faltered, closed it again.

Then said, 'I like the cover.'

'The aesthetics are by-the-by, Thomas.'

Howard shook his head like a teacher to a slow child.

'With this in his hands your predecessor was playing with elements far more dangerous than fire.'

He put the book on the desk, lying open to a certain page, littered with spidery script and sketchy diagrams. Taking one of the smaller notebooks he flicked through to an extract he had noted earlier.

'Here, see?'

He tapped a page, turned it towards Thomas.

'It's clear from this that he was intent on calling forth an agent of the dark powers.'

Thomas leaned in for a closer look, but Howard was already skimming ahead.

'And here,' he indicated. 'This would suggest that he had some measure of success.'

Thomas paused to take this in.

'You mean, he actually summoned a... something...?'

Howard pursed his lips.

'Euphemisms, Thomas,' he chided.

Thomas accepted the rebuke with a nod.

'A demon. He called up a demon?'

Howard waved a notebook.

'So he claims here.'

'Into this house?'

'This very room.'

'My God!'

Howard tutted.

'Not your god at all, Thomas,' he said. 'The deities worshipped by the peoples of the dark era were a very different bunch.'

The high ceiling tossed Howard's words back at them and Thomas shivered, though the room was warm.

'So, what happened to Richard Kirkwood?' he asked.

'That, I'm afraid, will require some further investigation.'

Howard arranged the books on the desk to best aid their studies, peering intently at the open pages.

'I wonder if I might be allowed to roll up my

sleeves.'

Thomas watched him already poring over the books.

'Figuratively?'

Howard tugged at the breasts of his jacket.

'Literally.'

'Please,' Thomas said. 'Be my guest.'

Howard slid off the jacket and hung it on the back of the desk chair then slowly and fastidiously he began to roll up his shirt sleeves.

Chapter Nine

Pulling the heavy curtains closed against the cool, dark evening, Thomas rubbed his eyes and stretched his aching back. He glanced at his watch, surprised at the passage of time since their investigation had begun; since his strange little guest had rolled up his sleeves. The eerie pressure in this room seemed not to bother the other man, hunched over the books, happily beavering away. But Thomas still felt it, as he had since that first day. A conflicting revulsion and attraction which had him returning to this place over and over, all the while desperate to leave. A headache threatened to grow behind his eyes and he shook his head to dispel it.

'It's late,' he said.

From his seat at the desk Howard barely glanced away from the ancient tome he was studying.

'Is it?'

He twisted the neck of the shiny new desk lamp to best angle the light onto its pages.

Thomas returned to the big chair, picking up the book he had rested open over the arm.

'I apologise for keeping you here so long.'

Howard smiled at his host.

'You might have had more trouble getting rid of me.'

Thomas laughed, turned another page.

'I admire your enthusiasm.'

'As I admire that of your ancestor.'

Howard's hand caressed the book.

'He was extremely diligent in his research.'

'I'm sure he'd be pleased he has a fan.'

'I don't dispute that I am.'

He picked up the sheaf of notes he had been scribbling during the long hours they had spent reviewing the book, and Richard Kirkwood's conclusions.

'His depth of understanding of the summoning terms is quite impressive.'

He swivelled in the chair, showing Thomas a face creased with concern.

'Although...'

'Problem?' Thomas asked.

'I fear there may be.'

'What is it?'

Howard slapped shut the Book of Shadows and picked up one of the notebooks bearing Richard Kirkwood's hand. He stood, as if to carry the notebook over to Thomas, but he remained by the desk, frowning over the words.

'As I say, there is a great amount of work amassed in these pages relating to the calling up of a diabolic entity, but...'

'You keep leaving your sentences hanging, Howard,' Thomas said, realising such carelessness was unlike him.

Howard slapped the back of his own hand.

'Dreadful of me, I do apologise.'

Thomas raised a hand, rejecting the apology.

'I'm less interested in your physical chastisement than in what those hanging sentences portend, my friend.'

Wide-eyed, Howard gaped at him.

'Friend?'

'Well?'

'Oh, yes, yes!'

Howard fought back the smile that the thrill of acceptance tried to beam from his face like a lighthouse lamp and forced his thoughts back to the matter at hand.

'Summoning is all well and good—'

He stopped, corrected himself.

'Well, not well or good at all, of course, but at least acceptable, if one has arranged a means of dismissal.'

'Dismissal?'

Thomas stood, took a step or two closer to the desk.

'How to get rid of whatever you've called up?'

Howard nodded eagerly.

'Precisely.'

'And Richard hadn't?'

Howard shrugged, turned back to the desk, began pulling open the drawers.

'Unless there are other journals you haven't yet shown me?'

'These are all there were.'

Howard's shoulders slumped.

'Oh dear.'

For a moment the two men stared at one another, pondering the implication of those words.

'You think,' began Thomas, 'that he may have brought something here from the depths of Hell and then not—'

Howard overrode his words.

'Or whatever dark dimension or infernal region he had accessed.'

He felt Thomas's gaze upon him.

'Let's not get swamped down in religious iconography,' Howard added, apologetically.

Thomas raised a brow.

'Oh, indeed, let's not.'

He cleared his throat and continued.

'But then, having done that, he'd not been

able to get rid of it?'

Slowly filling his lungs Howard then heaved a huge sigh.

'There is a distinct chance that such was the case.'

Thomas paced back and forth, ending up at the carved marble fireplace, hand resting on the cold mantelpiece.

'So, some devilish monstrosity has been walking the earth all this time?'

He turned back to Howard, fear in his eyes.

'Could even be out there still?'

'I do have to express doubts about that.'

Tugging at the creases of his trousers Howard resumed his seat.

'Had a creature of such power and evil intent been allowed to remain in society, I believe we would have heard more of him.'

Thomas perched on the arm of his chair.

'Good point.'

'You say you've studied these journals for a year?'

'Not exclusively,' Thomas explained. 'My son was in a serious accident, not long after I discovered this place. That took up a lot of my time and commitment.'

'Priorities,' Howard nodded. 'I understand.'

'Why do you ask?'

Snatching up one of the journals Howard trotted across to Thomas's side.

'There's something else here. I wondered if you'd noticed it.'

'What is it?'

The book shook in Howard's agitated grasp, blurring the words, and Thomas caught his wrist to steady his hand.

'Do these dates and names strike a chord, at

all?'

Thomas peered close, head shaking in bewilderment.

Howard pointed out the passages in question.

'Mary Kelly. Elizabeth Stride... and here, Mary Ann Nichols.'

He flicked through the pages.

'And more. And these dates, ranging through the latter half of 1888.'

'They ring a bell, but...'

Thomas shrugged, frowned, looked again.

'Five names, all prostitutes, viciously hacked to pieces in the worst backstreets of Whitechapel.'

Thomas stood, backed away from the smaller man.

'Are you saying...?'

His chest pounded and the headache attacked him afresh. Had a mystery that has confounded historians for over 130 years been unveiled before them, a secret uncovered that would astound the whole world? And, if so, how could they ever tell a living soul? After all, who would believe such insanity? Did he even believe it himself?

'Is it possible...?'

'Why would Richard Kirkwood have listed these foul murders in his journals,' Howard reasoned, 'unless he thought they were connected to the atrocity he had brought forth?'

'And when that series of gruesome killings ended so suddenly...?'

Howard flicked ahead through the journal, shaking his head.

'One can only assume that that was when the previous Kirkwood was finally able to find a way to despatch the thing back to the inferno.'

'Inferno?' Thomas laughed. 'A literary reference in place of a religious one?'

Howard was almost blushing.

'If you'll permit my indulgence'

'Certainly.'

He gave a small bow of the head, in acknowledgement of the favour.

'Thank you.'

'So it's definitely gone?'

Howard pulled a face, cautious optimism mixed with uncertainty.

'It's hard to be definitive when we only have speculation and century-old jottings.'

He looked around the room, hand held out, fingers feeling the air. He bent and touched the discoloured mark on the floorboards.

'And, of course, once a breach has been made, the wound never fully heals.'

'Breach?'

Thomas stepped further away from the chair.

'Like a doorway between our world and wherever this thing was from?'

Howard lifted a finger from the floor and touched it to his tongue, grimaced.

'That's right.'

'So it could come back?'

Howard sat suddenly in the chair, hands on the arms, holding his breath as if waiting for something to happen. After a moment he released the breath in a sigh.

'Not by its own devices but, with assistance, the passage would be easier to one who had travelled through such a breach before.'

Thomas strode over to the desk, picked up the Book of Shadows.

'Then, the prudent thing,' he said, closing the tome and staring at it earnestly, 'would be to destroy this book. And all the notes and journals. Eradicate all evidence of the thing's previous visit.'

He piled the books together on the desk.

'That way no one can be tempted to duplicate the summoning.'

He looked as though he might set a match to the heap there and then. But something, whether it was something within himself, or some exterior force, something stayed his hand.

'Prudent, yes,' said Howard, rising and stepping tentatively closer. 'One might even say sensible. But...'

Thomas turned to him.

'You're hanging again, Howard.'

Howard pondered his next words for a moment.

'We're both intelligent men, would you agree?'

'I would,' Thomas nodded. 'Intelligent. Prudent. One might even say sensible.'

'And, as such, may be considered wise enough to exercise caution when faced with temptation.'

'One would hope so.'

'And no one else is aware of the existence of these documents, I assume?'

'Not to my knowledge.'

Howard slipped past Thomas, placed a gentle hand on the pile.

'Surely the weight of their historic importance and informative value must be set against any danger inherent in their mere state of being.'

He turned imploring eyes towards the taller man.

'Wouldn't you say?'

'You think they're worth more, to history and to mankind, if we kept them?'

Howard spread his hands submissively.

'That would be my humble opinion, yes.'

Thomas stroked his chin.

'So, don't destroy them?'

Howard cocked his head, watching him.

'The notion troubles you?'

All the eerie sensations which had assailed Thomas's nerves this last year sparked into life again now. He felt again the chill of entering this house, the sense of presence upon entering this room. The need to be here fighting the desire to lock the door behind him and drop the key down the nearest drain. And all the while that unvoiced siren, calling him, calling him...

'You mentioned temptation,' he said.

Howard nodded sagely.

'Power is a potent aphrodisiac.'

'And a being such as could be summoned in this manner would be able to endow power upon the one who summons, beyond the imagination of any normal man.'

'They would.'

Howard pulled the Book of Shadows from the bottom of the stack, letting the smaller journals tumble onto the desktop.

'Are you feeling the tug?'

Thomas blinked at Howard, shook his head, mystified.

'Tug?'

'The pull that texts like this – powerful, attractive, magnetic – can exert over a person. It's to be expected. You're not familiar with the world of the occult and the supernatural. You've not studied them, trained with them. You're not so adept at denying the baser feelings that these things can stir up.'

Thomas turned his back on Howard, stalking across the room to the window and drawing back the curtain, cooling his wrists on the iron bars firmly attached there.

'It's more than a thirst for power,' he said. 'It's a desire for knowledge, for answers. Something dark and inexplicable happened in this room and I need to know what that was.'

'That's understandable.'

Howard put down the book and followed him to the window, reached out a hand towards his shoulder, then let it drop again to his side.

'But finding out could involve incredible danger.'

'I know.'

Thomas turned to face him again, fire in his gaze, jaw set in determination.

'Can you help me? *Will* you help me?'

Hands clasped before him, Howard let his eyes drop to the carpet, as if pondering the scuffed toes of his Oxford boots.

'Yes,' he said eventually. 'Yes, of course.'

'Excellent!'

Thomas's long legs took him swiftly back across the room.

'What do we need to do?'

Thomas had retrieved the book and was flicking through its pages.

'What, now?'

Howard scuttled to his side.

'No! We need to prepare. I have to fetch wards, apparatus, utensils.'

He waved his hands, fingers grasping at nothing.

'It's far more than a case of shouting names in the air and waiting for something diabolical to answer the call.'

Thomas threw down the book, shoved his hands in his pockets, huffed in frustration.

'I'm sorry, Thomas,' Howard said, 'but if we rush this then the consequences could be unimaginable.'

Thomas nodded, moved away from the desk.

'No, no, you're right, of course. You're the expert. I defer to your knowledge and experience.'

'Thank you.'

Howard seemed relieved.

'May I take this?'

He lifted the book. The old book, the Book of Shadows, the powerful book. Thomas felt a strange pang in his chest at the suggestion that the book should leave the premises.

'Maybe I can get some insight,' Howard continued, 'into the particular being we are dealing with and be able to forearm myself accordingly.'

Thomas was staring at the book, breathing harsh and strained. He raised a hand to snatch the book from the smaller man, but he fought it back to his side.

Howard caught the look, frowned.

'I can have it back as soon as tomorrow. We can very quickly be one step closer to the answers you seek.'

With an effort to control the inexplicable fury surging within him, Thomas nodded and made his way inelegantly to the chair.

'Take it, take it. You're right. Preparation, and a new approach, that's what's needed. We've been poring over these books for ages. Few hours rest and we can come back at it fresh tomorrow.'

'Wise words.'

Howard slipped the book into his briefcase, wrestling with an awkward buckle.

Thomas averted his eyes to avoid seeing the book disappear. This curious feeling disturbed him. He was usually so casual over possessions. It was just a book, let him take it. He's promised to bring it back. Logic winning over instinct, Thomas sighed, watching his breath turn to mist before him.

'Sudden chill,' Howard remarked, glancing round the room, his expression anxious.

'Yes,' Thomas said. 'There's a draught gets in here from somewhere. I've noticed it before.'

He rose from the chair and checked the latch of the window, pulling the curtain tight again.

'I expect that's it,' said Howard, though he didn't sound convinced.

They exchanged a few pleasantries as Thomas saw Howard to the door. The words meant little to Thomas though they left Howard with a beaming smile and a tear in his eye, but Thomas quickly forgot them as the oppressive atmosphere in the house clouded his mind with unformed dread. He considered grabbing his jacket from the hall, locking the door and shooting back to the estate right there and then, but immediately shrugged off the thought and made his way back up the narrow staircase and along to the study.

At the desk he gathered up the journals and notebooks and bundled them all into a drawer shutting it with a slam. For a moment the eerie sensation in the room lifted, a pressure slipping from his shoulders, the tension in his chest easing. Then, unbidden and almost against his will, his hand reached out and opened the drawer once more. He stared at the clutter of books, fear and desire fighting within him as he took out one of the one-hundred-and-thirty-year-old journals. Laying it onto the desktop the book fell open at a well-thumbed page and Thomas's eyes were immediately drawn to a passage in his ancestor's scratchy writing.

'*Maz sharat sha mashaz alamdak*,' he murmured, as the words swirled under his gaze. '*Mushu maz sharat alash.*'

He blinked, but couldn't tear his gritty, stinging eyes away from the book.

'*Maz sharat sha mashaz alamdak*,' he repeated, his voice becoming stronger. '*Mushu maz sharat alash.*'

Icy crystals formed on his quivering lips, his tears froze and cracked on his face. The words puffed from his mouth in ever-thickening clouds, the mist obscuring his vision. But by now the chant was embedded in his mind, and he continued the recitation without need of the journal, which dropped from his loose fingers.

'*Maz sharat sha mashaz alamdak. Mushu maz sharat alash.*'

Sweat trickled in streams down his back and his shirt clung to his flesh, despite the racking cold shuddering through him. In the churning mist now filling the enclosure a shadowy shape could almost, but not quite, be discerned. Keeping to the periphery of Thomas's sightline the figure, or substance, or unnameable thing hovered and circled, moving ever closer, growing ever more solid and distinct.

'*Maz sharat sha mashaz alamdak. Mushu maz sharat alash.*'

As Thomas continued to repeat the incantation a second voice mimicked him, its gravelly tone echoing around the chamber, the sharp consonants hissing like a pit of snakes being stirred with a stick. A presence, no more than a blur of motion and perception of being, crept up close behind Thomas, and arms as cold and relentless as shifting glaciers but ephemeral as clouds, wrapped around his chest, gently, tenderly, crushing the breath from him. Fingers soft as a lover's slipped between his ribs and touched icy tips to his heart.

As that heart juddered to a halt a dreadful realisation shook the dying man with the knowledge that he and Howard had got everything so very, very wrong.

Book Three

Luke Kirkwood

Chapter Ten

Light chamber music drifted through the rooms, and sombre, grey-haired men in dinner jackets clinked champagne flutes with elegantly-gowned ladies glittering in their finest diamonds. Luke Kirkwood kept his hands in the pockets of his jeans, making no attempt to disguise the huge yawn stretching his face.

'I know you find these occasions tedious, darling,' said his mother, 'but do try not to be quite so obnoxious.'

Emma Kirkwood outshone all her guests with her style and beauty, sailing amongst the crowd afloat a tide of casual sophistication.

A young woman in maid's uniform passed carrying a silver platter of cocktails. Luke grabbed two, downing one immediately and returning the glass to the tray before the girl walked on.

Emma shook her head.

'It's going to be one of those nights, is it?'

'These things are so dull,' Luke huffed. 'Same guests as always. Some mediocre string quartet droning out one baroque dirge after another.'

'They better not be mediocre, with the amount they're charging.'

'I wish you'd let me invite Kaitlyn.'

'Your dancer?' Emma shuddered. 'You've barely known her five minutes. You know nothing of her background, beyond the insalubrious premises wherein you made her acquaintance. We'd probably spend the whole evening stopping her climbing on the tables and throwing her underwear at the vicar. For all you know she might stab you in the back and run off with the silver.'

'You're such a snob, Mother.'

'Well, of course I am, dear.'

She patted his cheek.

'It's your own inverted snobbery and youthful rebellion that make you insist upon continuing this dubious relationship. But let's face it, she'd hardly fit in with this crowd, they'd eat her alive.'

Luke took a sip of his remaining drink before answering.

'She's stronger and brighter than you give her credit for.'

'That wouldn't be difficult, because I don't give her much.'

He pulled a face.

'Have you never heard the phrase "reverse psychology"? You're only pushing me into her arms.'

'In that case, she's wonderful. Ideal!'

Emma waved her hands grandly.

'I wholeheartedly approve.'

'Thank you, Mother, for giving us your blessing.'

He gave her a lopsided grin.

'I'll propose tomorrow.'

She sighed, but returned the smile.

'You're an absolute swine.'

'I blame the parents.'

'Yes, so do I.'

She raised her own glass and clinked it against his.

'Speaking of whom, I notice Dad snubbed your little *soiree*.'

Emma rolled her eyes and her fingers

tightened on the stem of her glass.

'So where is he?'

'Where do you think?' Emma sighed. 'At that new place of his in the City. Probably tupping several voluptuous wenches even as we speak.'

Luke laughed at the phrase.

'He's not having an affair, Mum. You know that.'

'Of course I do. I wish he were. It might take his mind off whatever this strange project is that's consuming him these days.'

'You're a strange old bird, aren't you?'

She rested a hand on her hip and looked him up and down.

'For wanting my husband's attention?'

'That's not actually what you said.'

She shrugged.

'Don't listen to what I say, only what I mean.'

He shook his head and laughed again.

'You're incredible.'

'You've noticed?'

They drank in contented silence for a moment, until Luke remembered how tedious this occasion was. He gestured with his empty glass, pointing out the sea of revellers surrounding them.

'God, look at them! Dead inside, the lot of 'em. Animated corpses shuffling around, spilling champagne on one another. It's the zombie apocalypse set to a Vivaldi score.'

'Then why do you come?'

'I live here.'

'You know what I mean.'

'Because you sulk if I don't.'

She pouted and turned her back.

'I do not.'

He groaned and ran his fingers through his

floppy hair. Much more of this and he'd be reduced to sticking cocktail sticks in his eyes, just to stay awake.

'I'm off,' he said, brusquely.

He put his glass on the window sill and headed for the door.

Emma followed after him, catching him in the hall.

'Where are you going?'

'I don't know.'

He ducked into the cloak room, rummaged amongst the gabardines and furs until he found his sports jacket. He checked the pockets for his car keys.

'Maybe I'll visit Dad. It's about time I saw this place of his.'

He held open the large front door as he said, 'Or I might go and see Kaitlyn, propose tonight instead of tomorrow.'

'Darling, you mustn't,' his mother called after him. 'You've been drinking.'

By the time Emma made it outside Luke's Lamborghini was churning up dust and gravel as it hurtled along the drive.

*

The country lanes are too narrow, the night too dark. Slow down, you idiot! Are you trying to kill yourself? Couple of drinks to ease the tedium of that miserable party, then getting behind the wheel – total lunacy. Too fast on that bend, the wall appearing out of nowhere.

A shattering impact, and noise to tear the mind...

Then there are flames, and the roar of grinding metal. Movement – fast, explosive, tumbling in the chaos, glass fragments cascading all around. Rolling endlessly – eternity in kaleidoscope. After eternity, shocking stillness as the fire rages higher, closer, wilder.

Hands, clasping around his chest, heaving him clear of the wreckage, dragging him safely from the blaze. Grass, dew-wet and chilly after the heat, prickling through his torn shirt.

He lifts his face from the dirt, twists to see his rescuer, to thank his saviour.

And looks into the face of terror!

The worst features of every horror movie monster smashed clumsily together in a single infernal entity. Flesh that could never have lived animated into a hideous snarl of anger and hatred. Livid scars, warty growths and bulging pustules mar every inch of visible skin jutting from beneath the tattered rags the thing wears. Its long, misshapen form looms above the young man, a man barely more than a boy. Barely more than the boy who first saw this face years ago and built a wall to keep it away.

A wall to hide behind.

A wall in his mind.

Then, years later, smashed a car through that wall and let it loose to stalk him once more. This creature with the name so ironically incongruous that merely to think it brings him to the verge of hysteria, yet he shouts it aloud, screams it with all the breath left in his gasping lungs, riding the harsh sound like a rolling wave as it hurls him bodily from the realms of nightmare and back into the waking world.

'Mister Nice!'

*

'Luke?'

He felt her hand, warm against the cold sweat on his shoulder.

'Kaitlyn?'

As the slow realisation of where he was dawned on him Luke Kirkwood blinked at her stupidly.

'I'm here,' she said. 'You're safe.'

'Am I?'

He shook his head to loosen the fading images, rubbed his face with his hands.

'Did I wake you?'

She smiled warmly and nodded at him.

'Don't worry about that. Are you okay now?'

'Yeah, yeah.'

He pulled the covers up over his shoulders and snuggled close against her.

'Want to talk about it?'

'No.'

'That's okay.'

She rested a hand against his face.

'Whenever you're ready.'

'I'm not sure I'll ever be ready.'

She caught a tear on his cheek with her thumb.

'Best not to keep things bottled up inside for too long.'

'I know.'

He sat up.

'Need to pee.'

He sat on the edge of the bath, felt the chill of the porcelain seeping into his bare buttocks, and he wondered how he could tell another human being about the thing from his nightmare. How could anyone possibly understand the distress these dreams conjured up, the dread they left behind? How could she, a sweet, naïve girl from somewhere up north, (she'd told him her home town many times but anything beyond Cambridge was untamed Badlands to him) possibly understand the stress he was under? All she needed was a stage or platform so she could stand up and wiggle her bum and all was well in her little world. He would soon be twenty-two – he'd seen something of life. Man of the world. He had stared Death in the face and turned away from the edge of the abyss. The bogeyman may be a figment of his darkest imagination, but the crash was real. And though scars fade and bones knit back together, there are some injuries worse than the physical ones. Almost a year since the crash but the night terrors still had their talons in him.

The door opened, Kaitlyn stood in the doorway, concern carving new lines on her pretty face. She wore that tiny nightie he'd bought her, which clung where it could while hiding just enough. Even leaning against the doorframe her legs were positioned for the perfect balance and her weight was on the balls of her feet, accentuating the lines of her calves and thighs.

'Are you coming back?'

'Babe!' Luke admonished. 'I might've been having a...'

He waved a hand at the toilet tucked tightly in the corner in the shadow of the cracked sink.

'I know every sound this flat makes,' she said, 'even over the noise of the traffic outside. I heard the bath creak as you sat down.'

This flat was seriously pokey. Tiny and dilapidated. No secrets in this place, not even from the neighbours. That thought had amused him on a number of occasions, as they had cavorted in Kaitlyn's squeaky bed. He'd promised to rescue her from this hovel many times, but her fierce independence kept her from accepting his charity. From their first meeting in that Soho nightclub fourteen months ago she'd stood her ground.

'No hand-outs.'

'What about that fifty I tucked in your suspender belt?' he'd reminded her.

'I earned that,' she insisted.

He smirked.

She scowled. 'Dancing!'

Their differences were obvious but they each fought to ignore them. From her look of surprise at the denomination of notes he shoved in her underwear, to his look of horror the first time she brought him to her flat, there had been a number of obstacles to overcome. His coddled upbringing, languishing in the Surrey residence and living off the Kirkwood fortune, made her journey from the suburbs of Manchester to a performing arts college in Enfield seem like the plight of the girl in the Hunger Games books. Apparently. She'd made the comparison, he'd never read them. Or watched the films. He liked to flirt with pop culture just like the common masses, but one had to draw the line somewhere.

College led to a brief placement in the chorus of *Phantom*, where she'd struggled to shine in the crowd scene during the *Masquerade* number, until the whole COVID thing had scuppered that opportunity. The club work subsidised her return to training but her dreams of the West End hadn't faded.

He took her to the Surrey rez once – she wouldn't touch a thing and had refused to go again. Though that might have had as much to do with the reception his mother had given her than her distaste for Chippendale furniture. Frosty didn't quite cover it.

Dad had been much more welcoming, God rest him. She did have a way of charming the men, he'd be just as susceptible as any. Perhaps that was Mother's objection?

Feeling strangely vulnerable Luke lifted a towelling robe from the hook on the bathroom door and pulled it on, then followed Kaitlyn back into the bedroom.

She was sitting on the bed, holding a hand out for him to join her.

'You'll feel better if you talk about it,' she said. 'Trust me.'

'I've talked about it,' Luke grumbled.

Months of talking to a kindly, round-faced woman, seated in comfy chairs, the bubble and hiss of a coffee machine as constant background static, had done nothing to eradicate the nightmares.

'Talking doesn't work.'

'I want to help.'

'I know you do, and I'm very grateful, honest I am.'

'Then let me.'

'You already do,' he said, taking her in his arms. 'You wouldn't believe how much it helps just being with you.'

'Is there nothing else I can do?'

She brushed his long, floppy fringe from his face.

'I'm a good listener.'

Those wide, earnest eyes appealed to him, and he felt compelled to offer some form of concession.

'Tell you what,' he said, 'come down to my

new place in the City at the weekend and I promise we can talk there. Less angst on fresh territory.'

'New place?'

'I've told you about it,' he said. 'The place my dad left me in his will. I'm taking my first look at it.'

She nodded and her face brightened.

'And you promise we'll talk then?'

'Promise.'

That seemed to appease her. He pulled aside the bed covers and they both wriggled back underneath, wrapping their limbs together like a sailor's knot. Within minutes he felt her breathing regulate and heard a faint rumbling emanating from the depths of her throat. It took him far longer to slip into another troubled slumber.

Chapter Eleven

She wasn't particularly religious, despite her parents' attempts at indoctrination, and had never considered herself superstitious, but even so Klaudia Nalewajka sent a silent, wordless prayer heavenwards and knocked heavily three times on the door before entering the room she knew logically must be empty, to disperse any malignant spirits which may be lingering within.

A man had died in this room. She hadn't been the one to find him, that had been the previous cleaner, a fierce Aberdonian woman who had taken a perverse pleasure in describing the scene in detail – the chill in the room on a warm day, the man's face, pale and twisted in the throes of agony and terror. For all her bluster she refused to return after that, perhaps understandably, but the contract remained in place so someone had to come and give the place a going over twice a month. And that duty had passed to Klaudia, who had trained as a secretary in Poland but earned more as a cleaner in London. She had chosen not to return home to Koźlina after Brexit, despite the attitude of so many of the people she met. She liked the UK, even if a large chunk of its population didn't like her. She had indefinite leave to remain, so she would remain indefinitely.

Most of the properties she had to deal with were considerably grimier than this one, barely furnished and left unoccupied since the death of the former resident. But she would rather face rats and rotting garbage than this sepulchral and sinister atmosphere. The downstairs rooms were swiftly dealt with, but this room, larger than the others and clearly more frequently used, offered its own set of challenges. For starters the door, which would initially resist attempts to open it then swing suddenly inwards, almost dragging her into the space within. The low temperature, whatever the weather outside. Noises, faint and indistinct, like whispered cries, going silent when she strained to listen.

She switched on the vacuum cleaner, letting its rattle and hum fill the room, drowning the aberrant sounds, leaving it to rumble to itself as she attended to the dusting. Bookcases first, then she took the feather duster to the shelves, holding it as near to the end of the handle as possible, to avoid touching any of the skulls and grotesque figures. Lastly, the desk. She always felt an overwhelming sense of awe and dread as she approached the bulky old item, hesitating before applying a quick squirt of polish and leaning in with the chamois. The incongruous pairing of an ornate antique quill alongside a pot containing biros and modern pencils struck her each time she reached them. She tipped out the pens onto the desktop so she could reach inside to dislodge any grit and dust which might have accumulated. As she collected up the pens to return them to their receptacle one of them eluded her, rolling away, disappearing down the back of the desk out of reach. She considered leaving it and moving on, but her pride wouldn't allow her to. On her knees she wiggled her fingers into the space between desk and wall, but the gap was too small, almost trapping her hand. With a firm shoulder she managed to heft the desk away from the wall to such an angle that she could crawl in behind. She found the pen amongst the fluff and detritus against the skirting board and thought that she really ought to fetch over the vacuum while the desk was out of the way, insert its hose and scoop away the muck, but that would add to the time she had to be here, when she was so close to finishing. It would keep until next time.

Pushing herself back out of the cramped enclosure she felt her tunic snag on the back of the desk, caught by a small knob or switch jutting from the otherwise smooth rear panel. Tugging to extricate herself she brought open a hidden drawer, from which tumbled a chunky, black handgun. She stared in dismay at the pistol lying on the carpet. The word Glock came into her mind, probably from watching too many American cop shows on TV.

Behind her the vacuum cut out unexpectedly, its off-button untouched. The droning whine faded to nothing. Into the ensuing silence the sibilant hiss, which she had almost convinced herself was the draft coming through the window frame, even though the breeze was mild outside, began to murmur its unheard message, urging her, persuading, beguiling.

Without wanting to she picked up the weapon from the floor, feeling the cool of the dark metal against her clammy palm. Without intending to she wrapped her hand around the grip, one finger hooking through the trigger guard. Without even the slightest desire to do so she turned the barrel towards her own face and inserted the open end of the barrel between her trembling lips. Her finger tightened fractionally on the trigger. Then tightened some more.

The hollow, empty click startled her back to her senses and she snatched the gun from her mouth, shocked and appalled at her own actions. She turned it around in her hands, noting the empty shaft in the butt of the handle where the magazine containing the bullets would be slotted to make the weapon viable. She thrust the gun back into its hiding place and shoved the desk back against the wall.

She swore to herself that she would tell no one of what had occurred – what had *almost* occurred – and to hand in her notice at the earliest opportunity. She would follow the exodus of her countrymen back to her homeland after all. The hell with remaining, she was definitely going to leave.

Chapter Twelve

'God, it's massive!'

Luke Kirkwood stared up at the pillared porch and the dirty brickwork looming above him and nodded his appreciation. He'd barely given a thought to the place his father had secluded himself away in all those nights he wasn't at home, but his mother's scornful remarks had conjured up images of a squalid den with dust and spiders.

'From the way you talked about it I was expecting a tiny garret or a filthy basement, not a whole sodding house!'

'Must you resort to vulgarity?'

'Fuck, yeah!' Luke said, giving his mother a sideways glance. 'What do you expect when you drop surprises like this on me? Must be worth a mill, easy.'

'Thereabouts, I would imagine.'

Emma Kirkwood dipped a hand into her Louis Vuitton clutch bag and produced the large key and offered it out to Luke, hooked on a slender finger.

'Here you go, Lord of the Manor.'

With a grin he took the key from her, weighing it in his palm.

'So it's really mine? Really, truly, all mine?'

'Indeed it is, Luke.'

She squeezed his shoulder and followed him as he approached the front door.

'All yours.'

He thrust the key into the lock proudly.

'To do with as I will?'

'Yes,' she said, then her voice took on a note of caution. 'Except sell it.'

He turned to her as the door creaked open behind him.

'What?'

He pouted sulkily, then, seeing his mother's smirk, he pressed on quickly before she could tell him how his expression reminded her of the time when he was two and she'd taken a worm from his mouth before he could entirely consume it. She loved repeating that one, especially in company.

'I can't sell my own house?'

'Not until you're twenty-five.'

'Twenty-five?'

He looked stricken, horrified.

'But that's forever!'

'Hardly.'

His shoulders slumped as he turned into the darkness of the entrance hallway. Bloody hell! What was the point of leaving him the place if he couldn't flog it on and pocket the cash?

In his huff he barely noticed the heavy atmosphere within the house, folding around him like an invisible fog.

Behind him his mother's heels clicked on the stone steps.

'Terms of the will,' she said. 'It's all written down.'

His bottom lip protruded.

'I didn't read it.'

'Perhaps you should.'

'It's morbid.'

'Of course it is. It's a will.'

It seemed she had perceived the eerie ambience, attributing it to a chill in the building, for she wrapped her arms around herself and shivered.

'But it's also your future.'

She wandered along the hall and popped her head through the nearest door.

'I wonder where the heating controls are...'

Ever capricious, Luke had already thrown off his funk.

'Don't you know the layout of the place?' he asked.

'I rarely visited.'

Her eyes were sad as they passed over the sparse furnishings and walls bare of art or decoration.

'This was your father's little hidey-hole.'

Close behind her he wrapped his arms around her, resting his chin on her head. She leaned against him, taking the comfort he offered.

'So it just stood here empty most of the time?'

'There are contract cleaners who come in occasionally, but otherwise yes, empty.'

He wandered off, calling to her from another room along the hall, voice echoing around the empty spaces.

'Not much here, is there?'

'I think your father spent most of his time in the study.'

'Where's that?'

'Upstairs, end of the hall.'

The rushed clatter of Luke's shoes on the uncarpeted stairs was followed by Emma's much more sedate footsteps.

He pushed open each door he passed along the upper corridor, glancing in as the doors swung away, shrugging at the largely bare bedrooms and meagrely equipped bathroom.

Then he was at the study door and he paused, pulled up short by a sense of eagerness, impatience, coming not from within himself but from beyond the heavy wooden barrier ahead. A lusty fervour, as of eyes leering ravenously, and for a moment he imagined he knew how Kaitlyn felt as she swung around a shiny metal pole in a dimly lit nightclub, hungry gazes assessing every curve and crevice. His vision swam and a building nausea swirled deep within him.

He started as a voice spoke close behind him.

'Are you all right?' Emma's tone was curious and concerned.

The bizarre sense of intrusion, of violation, was fading as quickly as it had struck, like a wave passing as he strode into the ocean.

'Did you feel that?' he asked breathlessly.

'What?'

Her hand stroked his back, a soothing gesture. He shook it off, ignoring the flash of anxious alarm in her eyes.

'Nothing,' he said, a little more sharply than necessary.

He reached for the handle of the study door, hesitant, as if he expected an electric shock, or something worse. Then he took a breath, twisted the handle and pushed on.

*

Emerging from Tower Hill tube station Kaitlyn Mondae bought a coffee from a mobile stall positioned opposite the entrance and, as she sipped the scalding brew, she checked the address on the note Luke had given her. He'd also given her money for a taxi but a swift glance at Google Maps on her phone suggested that it would be almost as fast to walk to her destination. She ignored the black cab parked at the corner of Trinity Square and headed off past the shiny black railings surrounding the impressive stone façade of Trinity House towards the intriguingly named Savage Gardens (named after former resident Sir Thomas Savage, a 17th century baronet, another quick search revealed).

The streets were not too crowded and the afternoon was mild so she hitched the strap of her holdall comfortably onto her shoulder and set herself a leisurely pace. It was a few days since Luke had stayed over at her flat and she was keen to see him again but he'd told her his mother would be there today and she was less eager to remake her acquaintance.

The way Emma Kirkwood's eyes travelled up and down her body on their first and so far only meeting had made Kaitlyn's skin crawl worse than a club full of lecherous drunks ever could. She understood that some mothers might be protective of their only child, especially if they had been involved in a near-fatal accident the year before, but the way Luke's mother had her claws so deep in her son was a bit, well, icky. Sure, they'd recently lost Emma's husband Thomas, Luke's father, quite suddenly and unexpectedly, but their bond had been a thing for a lot longer than that. And for all his apparent stabs at rebellion – visiting dubious nightclubs, taking up with a girl who is quite simply not one of us, darling – he couldn't quite bring himself to cut the apron strings. But Kaitlyn was working on it.

Her own family background was as different as could be. Six kids, to almost as many fathers, living with a single mum who was more interested in collecting the Social Security benefits than in creating a loving family atmosphere. In true Billy Elliot style Kaitlyn had received scant encouragement when the dancing bug bit and had needed to work hard to earn, and pay for, her place in a prestigious dance and stage academy as far from home as possible. She wasn't the best dancer in the world, but she was good. She had a shot, as they say. As her coaches and instructors said. But they would, wouldn't they? That was part of what she paid them for. Training and motivation. They weren't likely to tell her she was shit and she'd never make it in the industry. That she should pack it in and go home. Not while she could still manage their exorbitant fees each term.

No, shush Kaitlyn, she admonished herself. Pessimism and negativity had no place beneath her flowing blonde curls, she mustn't let them back in, not again. Not like after the pandemic struck and the theatres all closed, costing her the *Phantom* gig just as she was starting to be noticed. Negativity was a black dog she'd been forced to kennel up with, alone, for weeks on end. She might have packed up then, she might have gone home, except that her mother's last words to her echoed in her thoughts, drowning out the black dog's strident howling. 'You'll be back,' in that scornful tone, with that sour expression. No, Linda – she'd stopped calling her 'Mum' years ago – I won't be coming back to this little slice of Hell. She hadn't said the words aloud, simply picked up her tatty rucksack and turned her back, but she knew in the coldest depths of her heart that she would never see her mother again. She wouldn't be going home, and she held no illusions that her mother would make any effort to contact her. Not that she'd find it easy if she did try. The girl she would be looking for no longer existed. Kaitlyn Mondae had superseded Paula Collier on all legal documents the moment she left Moss Side's grim environs. The streets may not be paved with gold down here in the Capital but there was far less shit in the gutters.

Maybe she was envious of Luke's closeness to his mother, and her devotion to him. Their relationship was the antithesis of everything she had ever experienced. He had never lain awake at night waiting for the rattle of the bedroom door handle, or the creak of the chair wedged against it as a drunken weight pressed on it from the other side, because there was yet another 'uncle' living in the house. Did she resent their happiness because she had never known it herself? Perhaps if she made greater steps to be friendly then Emma Kirkwood would see beyond the rough edges and recognise the depth of the feelings Kaitlyn held for her son, and her abrasive attitude would soften.

Perhaps...

Chapter Thirteen

'I might move in,' Luke announced, a mischievous impulse spurring his words.

The apprehension which gripped him moments before had dissipated in the antique aura permeating the room. The skulls on the shelves grinned at him and the grotesque statuettes beckoned and welcomed him. The high ceiling and the panelled walls seemed to be pulling at him, drawing him out, making him taller, larger, feeding him, building him. It was a slightly intoxicating thrill and he felt giddy and elated.

'Move in?'

'Yeah, could be fun.'

He spun around, arms wide, his gesture taking in the whole room.

'My own little bachelor pad.'

'Leave home?'

Emma caught his hand, turned him towards her.

'That's a big step,' she said. 'Aren't you being a little impetuous?'

'I'm a big boy now. Property tycoon, and all that. Time to stand on my own two feet.'

'It's a big place, you'll be ever so lonely.'

He could see he was getting to her so decided to ramp up the torture level even higher.

'Kaitlyn's coming down later. She'll love it! I might ask her to move in.'

'You invited that girl here?'

'Keep calling her "that girl" and I'll start calling you "that woman".'

'You can't seriously be considering moving her in?'

Luke circled the Chesterfield armchair, stroking the leather, before lowering himself into it like an invader usurping a throne.

'Why not?' he asked, from his position of power. 'We've been together for a while now.'

'Barely a year.'

'That's a while.'

She approached the throne and he smirked as he imagined her dropping to her knee before him.

'You're far too young for that sort of commitment,' she said.

'Old enough.'

He thrust himself out of the chair.

'Old enough to do most things,' he added. 'Except sell my own house, it seems.'

He picked up a skull from a shelf, peering at it inquisitively, turning it over, poking a finger into the eye sockets.

'Your father didn't want you making any rash decisions,' Emma said. 'Think of it as an investment.'

'Investment?'

He glanced at her over his shoulder.

'It's old money, isn't it?'

He knew the place had belonged to his great, great, however-many-greats grandfather. A forgotten relic from which his father had only recently blown the dust.

'It's an investment as far as you're concerned.'

Emma moved to his side and hooked her arm though his.

'Saving for your future.'

'Whether I like it or not?'

He aimed the remark at the skull in his hand

and with a jerk of his wrist the skull nodded in sympathetic understanding.

'What's with all this weird shit, anyway?'

He held the skull so that it appeared to be looking at his mother.

'Was Dad a witch, or something?'

With a grimace of distaste Emma used a single finger to face the skull away from her.

'Hardly. This has all been here for well over a hundred years. Some ancestor of his had an interest in the occult, apparently.'

'Really?'

He grinned with relish, intrigued by the idea.

'Apparently so. Your father had found some old documents and was trying to decipher them. Madness, if you ask me.'

She shuddered and moved away.

Luke stared deeply into the skull's bony face.

'You're a wizard, Harry!' he announced, in a deep Scottish brogue.

Emma tutted and rolled her eyes.

Luke affected rich Shakespearean tones and held the skull aloft.

'Alas, poor yogurt!'

Emma sighed heavily.

'Behave!'

'Warlocks, Mother!' Luke said, making it a profanity.

'Put it down!'

Emma took the skull from him and returned it to its place, rubbing her hands together briskly.

'What's up with you?'

'It's obscene.'

Emma reclined on the *chaise longue*, draping an arm over the low back, placing a cool hand on her forehead.

'He's not bothered.'

Luke tapped the skull in an investigative manner.

'I think he's dead.'

'You're not funny.'

Emma closed her eyes and breathed slowly and deeply.

'This whole collection is revolting.'

Luke watched his mother's apparent distress and his cruel mood softened. He knelt by the *chaise* and eased off her shoes.

'So why did Dad keep it all?'

'God knows. I'll tell the cleaners to throw the whole lot away next time they come.'

'No, don't.'

She opened one eye and looked curiously at him.

'What? Why?'

'I like them.'

'Seriously?'

He rose and went over to a rack of shelves, fingers caressing a cross-legged carved figure with the head of a goat.

'They're part of the contents of the house, which means they're mine.'

He turned back to Emma with an affable smile.

'I'm going to keep them.'

'Oh, for goodness' sake!'

She curled up her legs and massaged her stockinged feet.

'Well, don't expect me to spend much time in this room while they're still here.'

'I didn't expect you'd be spending much time here at all,' he said. 'Aren't you desperate to get home?'

She stood and moved to him, arms around

him, up on tiptoes to rest her head on his shoulder.

'Are you trying to get rid of me?'

'Not at all,' he said. 'I just thought you'd be missing the luxuries of home.'

'Do you really want to send me back to that big, rambling place, all on my own, no one to protect me?'

Luke laughed.

'There are at least seven people in that house at any given time. Two more in the cottage. Not to mention the dailies.'

She leaned back so she could look in his eyes.

'Those aren't people,' she said. 'They're staff.'

He shook his head.

'Listen to yourself, Mum.'

She hugged him tightly, stroked his cheek.

'I nearly lost you last year,' she said. 'I nearly lost everything.'

'I'm still here,' he said, his voice warm, reassuring.

'Can you blame me for wanting to spend time with you?'

His grin was cocky, lop-sided.

'I don't blame anyone for wanting to spend time with me.'

She gave him a playful smack on the arm and went to retrieve her shoes.

'Besides,' he said, 'I won't be alone, remember? Once the delectable Kaitlyn arrives.'

She arched an elegant eyebrow.

'How could I ever forget?'

'Still, it's a large enough house. There ought to be enough room for two women to co-exist without it becoming a battleground.'

She beamed a grateful smile.

'So I can stay?'

He grinned wickedly.

'Just don't take the room next to ours. I wouldn't want the noise to keep you awake all night.'

She rolled her eyes, used to his teasing.

'You are such a little monster!'

He held out his arms to her.

'But you love me.'

She feigned momentary reluctance then entered the embrace.

'I suppose I must.'

'Speaking of rooms,' Luke began, heading out to the corridor, 'which one did Dad use?'

The first room at the top of the stairs, at the opposite end of the upper hallway, seemed to be the largest. There was a king sized bed of a modern design, made up with clean bedding. Luke realised it must the one his father had installed and used when he'd stayed over.

Emma entered behind him, looking around sadly at the room.

'Yes, this one.'

The bed sheets were folded to the foot of the bed to allow it to air, so she rolled them up and tucked them in. Her hand lingered on the closest of the pillows and Luke could see the memories clouding her eyes.

'I wish I'd stayed here more often,' she said. 'Spent time with your father while I had the chance.'

Luke put an arm around her shoulders.

'Oh, Mum.'

'Can't, now.'

'Don't.'

'He was still so young,' she said. 'No age at all. And to just drop down dead like that...'

'It could've happened any time,' Luke argued.

'With the heart there's often no warning.'

He sounded more confident than he felt. His father's death had come as a shock to them both. How had the doctors missed the signs? Or perhaps his father had kept it to himself? Fear of his impending death, or a desire to protect his family from what was to come, preventing him from confiding in them.

'I don't want to waste any time with you,' Emma said, placing a gentle hand on his face.

'I'm not going anywhere,' he assured her.

'I'm sure you'd have said the same thing last year.'

'I'm still here, aren't I?'

'You nearly died.'

'I did die.'

'Don't remind me!' she said, hand clutched to her chest. 'I was outside the room when the machine stopped beeping. Doctors and nurses racing around in a controlled panic. Zapping you with electricity. You can't possibly understand how that feels, seeing your own child like that.'

'It takes more than a fatal car accident to keep me down.'

'Don't joke about it.'

'I turned away from the light,' he said grandly, hand raised to an unseen beacon. 'Clawed my way back to the living. For you.'

He kissed his mother gently on the forehead.

'And maybe for Kaitlyn,' he added with a wink. 'I hadn't shagged her then. I was on a promise.'

She pushed away from him and strutted from the room. The sound of her heels clacking on the stairs reached him again.

'What's wrong?' he called, affecting an air of innocence as he trotted after her. He caught up with her in the kitchen, a large space, dimly lit due to its narrow windows and the neighbouring skyscrapers stealing the sunlight. The fittings in the room were old fashioned to Luke's view but not Victorian, probably added when the house had been renovated in the seventies.

Emma stood at the sink filling the kettle. She was trying her best to avoid his eyes.

'You are a bastard,' she said, but the tiny creases round her eyes and the moue of her mouth belied the severity of her words.

'You'd know,' he countered.

She clicked the switch on the kettle and searched the wall cupboards for cups.

'I should've sold you at birth.'

'No one could afford me.'

Her voice softened.

'You are so your father's son.'

'That's not what you just said,' he reminded her.

She tweaked his chin fondly.

'Same cruel wit,' she said.

'Aww,' he pouted. 'Am I cruel?'

She turned her back to him as she attended to the drinks.

'You treat me so shoddily.'

He laughed.

'You're no helpless punch bag,' he said. 'No one walks over Emma Kirkwood.'

She half turned to him and tousled his hair.

'Only you, my bonnie boy, only you.'

The kettle clicked off and Emma returned her attention to the mugs.

'It's instant, I'm afraid,' she said. 'Your father never did know how to look after himself properly.'

Luke wandered over to the nearest window,

peering out at the high-rise blocks looming above them.

'Less of the Hamlet, more of the Towers.'

'What was that, darling?'

Emma brought him a coffee. He jerked a thumb towards the window.

'Tower Hamlets.'

He reached towards the window catch.

'Don't open it,' she said. 'You'll have the whole place smelling of curry.'

He gaped at her.

'That has to be the most racist thing I've ever heard you say.'

She patted his cheek.

'You're still young, give it time.'

Taking his drink Luke sank onto one of the rickety wooden chairs at the Formica-topped table. The weird agitation which had gripped him prior to entering the study was almost entirely forgotten now, replaced by elation that this place, neglected as it was, belonged to him. That it had come to him through tragedy didn't escape him, but this pride of ownership filled his chest in a way nothing ever had before. He'd possessed flash cars and smart clothes aplenty, gifts from his parents as, in a way, was this, but they were ephemeral, disposable. This house was permanent, enduring, it would outlast him. The initial impulse to sell it had been foolish and immature, he could see that now. He'd grown in the short time since they passed through that creaky door. He needed this house and, strangely, perversely, a whispering voice deep in his subconscious told him that it needed him, too.

Emma watched him, reading his thoughts.

'You're not really planning on living here, are

you?' she asked. 'It's hardly the most salubrious part of the City. I can't see you rubbing shoulders with the hoi polloi on a daily basis, talking like someone from that awful television programme.'

'You ain't my muvvah!' he said, in a thick, high-pitched cockney accent.

She shook her head.

'I sometimes wonder.'

They both chuckled at the shared joke, then she joined him at the table and they sat for a moment in companionable silence, sipping their drinks.

A cheerful chiming broke the moment. An extract from some classical piece, Luke guessed, knowing his father's tastes, but the sound was modern and incongruous in the sombre, old building.

'That's the door,' Emma said, unnecessarily. 'The hi-tech security thing. Computerised whatnot.'

'I'll have to get it synced to my phone,' Luke said.

'I expect it's your young lady-friend.'

The sneer was obvious in her voice.

'I'll go and let her in.'

'No point waiting for the butler to do it.'

Luke opened the door and Kaitlyn skipped up the steps into his arms.

'Hello, you,' she said, pressing her mouth over his.

He crushed her in his arms.

'So good to see you,' he said. 'You found it all right, then?'

She looked over his shoulder, wrinkled her nose.

'So, this is it, eh?'

'Not impressed?'

'It's big...'

Luke caught the hesitation.

'But...?

'Well...'

She slid past him into the hallway, looking around. As Luke closed the door behind her the corridor grew dark and she winced as a tremor ran through her body.

'It's a bit...'

'Bit what?

'Grotty.'

'Grotty?' he repeated, incredulous. 'It's a three-bed in E1, for goodness' sake!'

He spun around, indicating the rooms off the hallway, the stairs, the height of the ceiling.

'I'll be minted,' he added. 'Once I can sell it.'

'Just thought it'd be nicer,' she said. 'The other place is fab, this is creepy.'

Luke struggled to disguise his disappointment.

'It was empty for ages,' he shrugged. 'No one knew it existed. Dad used it for... whatever he did here.'

Then he grabbed her, held her, attempted to share his enthusiasm with her.

'It needs a bit of work, granted, but think of the potential.'

'What did you mean,' she asked, 'when you said "once I can sell it"?'

'Oh, complications,' he said, dismissively. 'Tell you later.'

There would be ample opportunity to get into the technicalities of his father's bequest, rather than the moment she walked through the door.

Her expression was troubled.

'It feels wrong,' she said.

'What does?'

'This house.'

'Wrong? How can a building feel wrong?'

Could she be experiencing that weird trepidation that struck him in the moment before he entered the study upstairs? That had been a momentary aberration, quickly shaken off. She'd soon come around, as he had, and accept the place as home.

'Is your mum here?' Kaitlyn asked, apprehensively.

'Yeah, in the kitchen.'

Luke pointed down the hall.

'I ought to go and say hello.'

He could tell she was merely being polite, that the notion of making pleasant chit-chat with his mother filled her with dread.

'Nah,' Luke said. 'There'll be time later.'

He took her hand, led her up the stairs.

'Let me show you our room.'

She followed meekly.

'Later?' she asked. 'Is she staying?'

'For now.'

'Oh,' said Kaitlyn. 'Great.'

Chapter Fourteen

Luke's offer to give Kaitlyn the full tour of his new domain had been declined with the excuse that she was worn-out from her journey and just wanted a breather in their room. Later, she'd promised, and he'd conceded and they settled down for a cuddle on the bed. The respite was brief, though, as even she agreed that they couldn't leave Emma alone for too long.

They had food delivered and drank one of the bottles of wine that Thomas kept for when he'd stayed over in the house. The afternoon passed slowly. Conversation was awkward and stilted. Emma's barbed comments failed to catch in Kaitlyn's flesh, partly due to Luke's warning that his mother enjoyed playing games to which she would eventually learn the rules, but also because Kaitlyn was too distracted to pay much attention.

Gradually the meagre light coming from the windows faded and they were forced to resort to switching on the lights. It was Emma who tired of the badinage first, blaming a budding headache, and she went up to the room she had chosen as her chamber for the night.

Kaitlyn washed up the few plates and cutlery they had used. Luke swished a tea towel around – playing peekaboo with it, wearing it like a scarf, flicking Kaitlyn's backside – and left the pots to dry on the draining board.

'Come on,' he said, when she'd dried her hands, 'let me show you the study.'

He almost had to drag her up the stairs, her

reluctance evident as they travelled the upper corridor towards the forbidding room.

'What's in there?' she asked, hesitating at the door. Luke hadn't mentioned his own experience of earlier in the day, so the foreboding she felt as the doorway loomed before them she dismissed as nerves from being in a strange place, far from home, with a man she believed she loved and his mother whom she believed hated her.

'Just stuff,' Luke said. 'Wee-ird stuff!' He drew out the word, making it sound creepy.

'What kind of weird?'

'You'll see.'

'I don't think I want to.'

'Come on, silly.'

He took her hand, went through the door, coaxed her in with a smile and a wink.

A shudder shook her as she passed through the portal, as if hands other than Luke's were on her flesh, eyes other than his were leering at her slender form.

'You okay?' he asked.

It wasn't real, she told herself. Just imagination. This house had a spooky vibe but that was just the dim corridors, the creaky front door, the old fashioned décor. It wasn't a horror movie set, it was just a house. Nothing more.

Luke had left the room in darkness as they entered but now he flicked the switch and the chandelier bloomed into life and she was able to see the skulls and grotesque statuary adorning the walls and shelves.

'What the hell?!'

She tried to step back but Luke had positioned himself between her and the doorway.

'Don't worry,' he said. 'They don't bite.'

'Are you sure?' she asked, moving warily into

the room.

He pointed out one skull, brown with age, curious symbols carved into the bone. It had no lower jaw and most of the upper teeth were missing.

'Well, *he* doesn't.'

'What are they? Why are they here?'

'Just souvenirs, decorations.'

'Decorations? It's not Hallowe'en.'

She wanted to turn and run but held her ground. He'd already called her silly for hesitating at the door. How ridiculous would she appear if she fled at the sight of a few gruesome artefacts?

'I think one of my ancestors used to be a witch,' he told her, rather proudly.

'What?'

Sitting reverently in the swivel chair he stroked a hand across the leather inlay of the desktop.

'He probably sat here, working on his spells.'

'Are you serious?'

'According to Mum, yeah.'

Luke opened the drawers of the desk and began rummaging around.

As she watched him, childishly excited, his attention fully upon whatever he was pulling from the drawers, Kaitlyn formed the impression that he was more interested in the room than in her. She wondered if he only brought her here as an excuse, so he could explore to his heart's content, without being accused of deserting her. Given a choice she would have sat alone in their room all night rather than spend a moment in here.

'Told you! Look,' he said, lifting his prize into view.

It appeared to be a collection of dusty notebooks, worn and old.

'What are they?'

'I reckon these are great granddaddy Kirkwood's spell books.'

'What, stage magic?'

She knew it was wishful thinking, even as she asked the question.

'Like rabbits out of hats?'

He gave a grim chuckle.

'I think it went a tad beyond that sort of thing,' he said.

He was flicking though the pages as he spoke.

'There's mention here of summonings, pagan rituals and other spooky shit.'

'You're kidding.'

'No, it's all here. It talks about conjuring something up. And a "Book of Shadows", whatever that is.'

There was a more modern, spiral-bound jotter amongst the older journals. Luke became engrossed in the scribbled entries.

'This is Dad's notebook,' he said. 'Looks like he was trying to make sense of it all.'

'And it wasn't just some sort of joke?' Kaitlyn asked. 'He was actually taking it all seriously?'

He turned the book so she could see the page.

'I guess he must have been,' he said, 'because he used a *lot* of exclamation marks.'

Kaitlyn was stunned. The notion that someone as sensible and intelligent as Thomas Kirkwood could give credence to such insanity was astounding. And a little frightening.

'I don't like it,' she said. 'Put them away. Let's get out of here.'

'Not yet, it's just getting interesting.'

'Please, babe. This room gives me the creeps.'

She rubbed the back of his neck. That could always distract him from whatever was on his mind. Except tonight.

He shrugged her off.

'Why don't you go and warm the bed?' he said, taking his eyes from the journals long enough to give her a cheeky wink. 'I'll only be a few minutes.'

'Promise?'

'Of course.'

He lifted her hand, kissed it, patted her behind.

'I'll not be long,' he said.

She leaned it, kissed the top of his head and ruffled his hair.

'Five minutes,' she said, with a note of insistence.

'Five minutes,' he repeated, but his mind was clearly back on the books.

She hated to leave him but the opportunity to escape this oppressive room was irresistible. If she had the strength to drag him out of here then she believed she would have tried, however crazy he might have thought her. But he'd follow her soon. He'd promised.

'I'll be waiting,' she said, in her most tempting, alluring voice, but she was talking to the back of his head.

'I'll be there soon,' he said.

Then, finally, he twisted in the chair and gave her another of his bold winks.

'Don't start without me.'

That, at least, was more like the Luke she knew. Relieved that he hadn't completely forgotten her she took her chance and all but ran from the room.

The mere act of passing the doorway was a

huge relief and she slowed her pace and took a deep breath.

As she passed the room to which Luke's mother had retired she paused and listened. Silence. And no light visible in the crack beneath the door.

Good. Being overheard at night with Luke at her flat didn't bother her at all, but the thought that Emma Kirkwood might be listening to their bedtime antics horrified her.

She quickly showered, doused herself in the expensive perfume that Luke had bought her and slipped naked between the cool, crisp sheets.

There was just a small bedside lamp illuminating the chamber and, filtered through the thin shade, it cast a warm, pink glow over the room. She spread her hair on the pillow like angel wings and waited for her man to join her.

And waited.

*

Fascinating!

Working through his father's notes, and referring to the musty journals of their shared ancestor, Luke had gleaned that the earlier Kirkwood's aim had been to summon some sort of benevolent entity from another realm to grant his desires. Sort of like calling up a genie without having to rub a dirty, old lamp.

Richard Kirkwood had been completely earnest in his campaign, as far as Luke could make out, dedicating decades of his life to the project, and Thomas appeared to have given credence to the ambition, if not to the ability of his antecedent to carry out his plans.

Turning to yet another passage in the dusty journals Luke came across a curious phrase written prominently across the page. The words were in no language he was aware of. Arabic, Turkish, Egyptian, they were all Greek to him. Staring at the ink scratchings on the age-browned paper afforded no clues so he attempted to vocalise it, carefully enunciating each word. He spoke at first under his breath, then louder, enjoying the way the phrase sounded in his voice.

'Maz sharat sha mashaz alamdak. Mushu maz sharat alash.'

He became aware of a soft, sibilant sound in the air around him, almost like the whisper of a naughty child mocking him. He assumed it must be a breeze disturbing the night outside and he checked the window was securely closed, allowing no draught to enter.

Returning to the books he repeated the incantation he had found, relishing the unusual syllables, rolling them round his mouth.

'Maz sharat sha mashaz alamdak. Mushu maz sharat alash.'

Again the hushed whispering, this time as if someone in the distance was calling his name, soft and slow.

'Lu-uu-uke...'

'Is someone there?'

He looked about the room, glanced out into the corridor.

'Kaitlyn?'

The hallway was empty, and he saw no one lurking in the darkness around him. Dismissing the uneasiness that had prickled his scalp as foolish and irrational he resumed his oration, firm and strong.

'*Maz sharat sha mashaz alamdak. Mushu maz sharat alash.*'

Over and over, the intonation rich and proud.

'*Maz sharat sha mashaz alamdak. Mushu maz sharat alash.*'

This time so captivated in the recitation was he that he failed to notice the shifting of the shadows in the corners of the room, the dimming of the lamp on the desk, the myriad eerie voices which joined his, subtly echoing the mystic chant.

Chapter Fifteen

Kaitlyn awoke, unaware that she'd been sleeping. Vague, ill-formed images danced in her subconscious and she realised she must have been dreaming. The memories flitted out of reach as she snatched at them and she allowed them to drift away, sensing that whatever scenarios played in her head would only disturb and upset her if she were able to recall them.

Sitting up in the bed the sheet fell to her waist and her skin tightened in the chill. The atmosphere was cooler now, the dim light more melancholy.

Had someone called her name? She was still alone in the bed – surely Luke's five minutes must have expired long ago.

Rising, she pulled a silky robe over her nakedness and, satisfying herself that he hadn't slipped into the room while she was dozing and was currently in the bathroom going about his ablutions, she headed out into the hallway.

The corridor seemed darker, more sinister even than it had when she first traversed it brief hours ago. It stretched before her, long and gloomy, disappearing into shadow. She flicked on the wall switch but the bulb buzzed and crackled, spewing out a weak, insipid sheen, drenching her in its sickly yellow light.

What was that noise from the room ahead? Weird chanting, unfamiliar words. Was that Luke's voice? The sound unnerved her and she faltered, ready to return to the bed, huddle down under the covers, wait for Luke to join her in his own time. When he'd finished... whatever it was he was doing in there.

But this was her man, her lover. What had she to fear from him?

The door stood slightly ajar as she approached and she leaned in close to listen and peep through the gap. Luke stood in an almost comically theatrical pose, back straight, one arm outstretched, other hand holding an old book up in front of his face, one of the journals from the desk. He was reading from the book, his voice sonorous, echoing round the high-ceilinged room. Or was that more than echo? It was as if other voices had joined his and intoned the unknown words along with him. But he was alone in the room. Wasn't he?

Kaitlyn pushed open the door and stepped inside, glancing around, seeking the source of the other voices.

'Luke?'

Luke gasped and dropped the book, dragged from an apparent stupor. He blinked at her as at a stranger. The other sounds faded as Luke ceased his recitation and the glazed look gradually slipped away from his eyes.

'Kaitlyn?'

'What are you doing?'

'Don't sneak up on me like that!'

Luke strained to control his breathing as he stooped to pick up the book.

Her concern glowed in her eyes.

'Are you all right?'

'Of course, I'm just...'

He waved the book vaguely, unable to form a coherent answer, then dropped it onto the desk. Kaitlyn moved to him and he took her into his arms; she gratefully melted into his warmth in the cold room.

'Hey, silly,' he said as she shivered against him, 'everything's fine.'

'What were those words?'

Face pressed against his chest, she felt his shrug.

'What words?'

He avoided her eyes as she peered at him.

'You were saying weird—'

He extricated himself from her grip, cutting off her questions.

'Nothing.'

'I heard you.' Her voice was barely more than a whimper. 'It scared me.'

'I was just... reading aloud.'

He cupped her face in his hand; it felt damp against her cheek.

'Nothing to worry about.'

'You're acting strange,' she said. 'I'm bound to worry.'

He wrapped his arms around her again, pulled her in close. The familiar strength of his embrace recalled to her mind their last night together. His disturbed sleep, his dark dreams.

'You said you'd tell me about your nightmares,' she reminded him.

'What, now?'

'You promised.'

He sighed and she felt a shudder run through him.

'I did, you're right.'

He drew her to the large leather chair near the cold, dark fireplace. He lowered himself into it and pulled her onto his lap. She felt a thrill buzz through her as she sat, and hoped it was merely reaction to the closeness of her lover, rather than the malevolent force her anxious mind suggested it might be.

'Relax,' he said, but it seemed like he was saying it to himself as much as her.

He stroked her hair and she snuggled close against him.

'Are you sure you want to hear this?'

'Tell me,' she said.

'It goes back to the accident,' he began, 'and further back. Much, much further.'

He paused and she sensed the turmoil within him as he dredged up the memories from deep in his psyche.

His mother's cocktail parties had been a feature of Luke's life since his earliest childhood, when he was a trophy to be displayed and passed around. A toy for his parents' friends to wind up and let go, to provide amusement for all.

Bitterness tainted his words as he told of one particular night when he was about eight years old. He was given a cup of punch by some wit or other and had to be carried to bed. He'd awoken in the early hours with a pounding head and a raging thirst. He went downstairs, looking for his mother or any responsible adult.

The last stragglers at the party had gathered in the parlour. They had turned off the lights and lit a few candles and were telling each other ghost stories like a bunch of silly teenagers on a camping trip. Unseen, Luke had sneaked into the back of the room and hidden in the shadows, listening to the gruesome nonsense being passed around.

Someone, Luke couldn't remember who after all this time, had told a tale of a being who had escaped, or been conjured up, or somehow made its way from the depths of Hell and ended up in

Siberia, or the North Pole, or somewhere equally chilly and inhospitable. The details had clouded in his memory but one thing remained sharp and clear. The storyteller was being flowery and evocative and had described the forbidding terrain as 'the land of mist and ice'.

Luke's sleepy, tipsy, eight-year-old brain misheard the quote and interpreted it as 'The Land of Mister Nice'. Even at such a tender age the irony of a hell-spawned creature having a name like Mister Nice wasn't lost on him, so it stuck in his head, and the first spate of broken nights started right then.

He'd grown out of it by about ten or eleven but the disconcerting visions had remained, buried and hidden, lurking in his subconscious ever since.

Waiting for the chance to resurface.

Luke had mentioned the accident to Kaitlyn, of course. Talked about the horrific crash and how he had died on the operating table. But on previous tellings he'd played down the seriousness of it, joked about dicing with death.

Now he told her of the monstrous creature who haunts his dreams, looms above his shattered form as the flames crackle around him, lifts him in gentle arms from the burning wreckage of his overpowered car. And carries him to safety.

He finally spoke of the scarred and twisted face that terrified a small boy and, years later, returned to defile the dreams of the adult he had become. A visage only a nightmare could spawn, atop a lumbering, misshapen tower of warped limbs, whose huge, grasping hands showed unnerving tenderness when laying him on the grass, clear of the churning blaze.

'But he's not real,' Kaitlyn said.

She stroked his face, kissed his forehead.

'Just a bad dream.'

'You think so?'

'Of course,' she said. 'Don't you?'

He sat, eyes closed, breathing deep and heavy, and for a moment she wondered if, during all this talk of nightmares, he'd drifted off to sleep.

Until his voice came to her, soft, almost a whisper.

'You know how they talk about, when someone dies, there's a light that represents Heaven, or whatever's waiting for you?'

'Yeah?' Kaitlyn nodded.

'It's true,' he said. 'I saw it.'

He hesitated again, and she saw sweat beading just below his hairline and noticed how pale he looked in the dimness of the room.

'It's all muddled now,' he continued, 'mixed up with the nightmares, but I do remember walking towards it.'

She wanted to stop him, tell him she'd changed her mind, that she didn't want to hear about the nightmares after all. But she could see that it was far too late. That now he needed to finish what he had begun. So she remained silent and listened.

'It was pulling me,' he said, 'drawing me closer and closer. I was about to be swallowed up, dragged through, but something – I don't know what – family? Thoughts of you? Fear of what was waiting beyond? Maybe even a force on the other side, pushing me away? I can't say, but something turned me around. And I came back.'

'Good.'

'Is it good?'

She smiled at him, but the cold blankness of his returning stare melted her smile away.

'Because there's this feeling – a premonition, or weird sixth sense, I don't know – but something tells me...'

His voice faltered, he croaked, licked his lips.

'... I didn't come back alone.'

*

Luke sipped the brandy he'd poured from the decanter his father had kept in the cabinet in the corner.

Kaitlyn still sat in the chair, legs curled up beneath her, robe pulled tight around.

'And you've been having these dreams for a whole year?'

'Pretty much.'

'God, Luke, that's—'

'Insane?' he interjected, his expression sour. 'Why do you think I've not wanted to tell you?'

'I was going to say it's terrible,' she said. 'You shouldn't have to go through that alone.'

He laughed, harsh and bitter.

'Oh, there have been plenty of people to talk to – my parents, therapists – but none of them really listen.'

The clink of decanter against tumbler rang out as Luke splashed another generous measure into his glass.

'I'm listening.'

'But you're not really hearing what I'm saying.'

'Of course I am.'

'No, you're like Mum and Dad, all you hear is *I've had a bad dream, pity me!* And all the doctors heard was *patient suffering from dreadful trauma, resulting in nightmares and delusions.*'

One hand pulling at his hair Luke stomped across the floorboards, eyes wild, staring at nothing.

Kaitlyn rose from the chair and put her arms round him, halting his pacing.

'Hush, baby.'

He shook her off, spun around, glaring into the shadows.

'I can feel him, Kaitlyn.'

His quavering voice held fear and a tear shone on his cheek.

'He's not just here, in my head.'

A knuckle rapped his forehead.

'He's in this house. In this bloody room.'

'Then come on, let's get out of here.'

She took his hand, pulled him towards the door. But his feet remained where they were.

'He won't let me go.'

'It's this crap on the shelves,' Kaitlyn said, crossing to the wall, snatching a hunk of stone, like a large pebble with a pentagram carved into its surface, from the mantelpiece.

'Leave it.'

'Get rid of it all and maybe you'll be able to find some peace.'

Before she could hurl it into the fireplace she screamed and the stone fell to the floor with a thud.

'What's wrong?' Luke asked.

'It burned me!'

'What? How?'

'It's hot.'

She showed him her hand, red welts forming a rough star on her palm.

'That's incredible!'

'I'm glad you're impressed,' she whimpered, 'but it sodding hurts.

'I'm sorry,' he said. 'I'll get something to dress it.'

He shook off the stupor which had seized him and rushed out through the door in search of bandages and ointment.

Kaitlyn blew gently onto her sore palm. Her next breath hovered visibly in the air and a sudden chill in the atmosphere sent a shudder through her. She pulled her nightgown tighter around her, rubbing her arms for warmth. Back to bed, she thought. Get under the blankets.

But she couldn't reach the door.

Her feet refused to move in that direction, keeping her rooted to the spot. A distant music drifted through the night, soft and eerie, creepily compulsive. At once liltingly mild and piercingly strident, it caressed her soul with soothing fingers while it raked her nerves with razor-like talons.

She swayed in time with the pulsing rhythm, feet shuffling on the bare boards, arms swinging at her sides. Her head bobbed and tilted, long hair flicking about, and hands no longer her own peeled off the robe and cast it across the room.

Goosebumps on her pale skin went ignored as the melody swamped her awareness, taking command of her flaccid limbs. Her movements at first were slow and lethargic, as if she was sleepwalking, body weaving like the smoke from a recently snuffed candle, but gradually her actions became more deliberate and energetic. The dance was free and wild, the music in her head throbbing, building, pounding its urgency into her like a passionate lover. Arms and legs swept around in wide swirling motions, erratic and feral but somehow hypnotically beautiful.

'Kaitlyn?'

Luke stood in the doorway, staring in bewilderment at the sight before him. His girlfriend, eyes closed, dancing naked like a mad woman to a harmony only she could hear. To him the only sounds in the room were the shuffling of Kaitlyn's bare feet and her quick, rasping breaths.

Her face was vacant, lost in some ecstatic dream.

He called her name again, the water-soaked face flannel he had brought for her falling from his grip, hitting the floor with a splat. He made to move to her, to comfort her, to stop her manic gyrations, but invisible hands held him back, unseen rivets nailed his shoes in place.

She danced on, oblivious to his return.

'Kaitlyn!' he wailed once more.

Now, at last, she noticed him there. Her eyes blinked open and shock, puzzlement and fear took turns usurping her visage.

But she didn't stop dancing.

'Luke?'

Her eyes caught his for the briefest moment, pleading and afraid, then she spun away again, her motions escalating, wilder and crazier than ever, building up a fierce crescendo.

Then, with a loud crack, as of something hard and vital suddenly, horribly snapping, Kaitlyn stopped, frozen in an awkward pose and, with a final, desperate look at Luke, she dropped heavily to the floor.

'Kaitlyn?'

Freed from his rigid stasis Luke rushed to her, collapsing to his knees at her side. He lifted her limp form, cradling her in his arms.

'Kate? Babe?'

She hung in his grasp like a rag doll, eyes

open but blank and lifeless. He stared at her, his face distraught.

Chapter Sixteen

'Have they gone?' asked Detective Inspector Michael Penn, leaning forward in his chair, elbows on the desk.

Across from him Detective Sergeant Debbie McDougall pulled the bobble from her ponytail and ran her fingers through her wild red hair, raking her blunt, bitten-down nails across her scalp.

'Aye, that sleekit solicitor was gettin' antsy, or I'd have kept the wee gobshite a while longer.'

Penn rubbed his face, feeling the drag of slack skin beneath his eyes, the rasp of bristles round his jowls. It had been a long day.

'You think he did it?'

'Nothing else makes any sense.'

Penn shuffled papers on his desk, pulled out the pathologist's report.

'The findings are inconclusive,' he said. 'No bruises or signifiers to suggest any physical force was applied.'

McDougall grumbled something unintelligible and rested one Dr Marten clad foot on her other knee.

'We're supposed to accept that she snapped her own neck?'

'There's no evidence that he caused the injury.'

'Except there was nae one else there, he admits as much hissel', and spinal fracture is a bleddy strange way to commit suicide.'

'That's true.'

Penn leaned back in his chair with a creak of

leather and a rattle of castors.

'But,' he continued, 'how do you explain how a young fella like that, barely six stone wet through, could inflict major internal trauma without leaving a mark on her?'

'Ah cannae,' she admitted, lips pulled back in a snarl. 'But that tale he telt 'bout her dancin' like a mad yin then droppin' down deid – are you buyin' that?'

Even after twelve years in London, McDougall's Glaswegian brogue thickened like tar when she felt wound up.

'Nae traces of drugs in her system,' she continued. 'So why the hell would she be actin' like she was aff 'er heid? I cannae explain it, you cannae explain it and, most significantly, he cannae explain it.'

Penn sighed. The interview had been prolonged and arduous, delayed by the solicitor's insistence on awaiting medical clearance that the lad was fit to be interviewed. The shock of seeing a loved one die in front of you is obviously distressing. Unless, of course, you were the perpetrator of the incident.

'He did stick to his story,' Penn argued. 'Even in the face of the Weegie onslaught. There aren't many who wouldn't at least waver a little.'

'And how widnae?' she growled. 'Just because he didnae swither doesnae mean he didnae do it, but.'

Penn watched her fidgeting hands as he took a moment to translate her growled phrases. The ballpoint pen she twisted in her white-knuckled grasp was in imminent danger of shattering. He read the thoughts behind the flaring green eyes.

'You can't live in the past, Deb,' he said. 'Gone are the days when a heavy hand could persuade a confession out of someone. Going in all guns blazing could lose us any chance of a conviction.'

'Ah ken that. He was always gunna be a tricky yin tae reel in. The slick wee fud would expect Mummy and Daddy's money to get him oot any trouble.'

The inspector frowned at his sergeant.

'Are you sure that's not just inverted snobbery?'

'Ach, awa'!'

She stood and stomped to the door.

'He might have you fooled,' she threw back over her shoulder, 'but Ah'm gonna be keepin' a keen eye on thon laddie.'

*

Rain thrummed heavily onto the umbrella and streamed down the flimsy nylon canopy, waterfalling around them in torrents.

Emma Kirkwood sidled closer to her son, linking her arm through his. He felt her pressure against his side, the only warmth on this unseasonably chilly day.

Typical funeral weather.

Emma looked striking in black as the small group stood in the grounds of the gothic-style, 19th century church, huddled against the elements amongst the crowded headstones.

At the edge of the scattering of mourners Luke spied the untamed ginger mane of the angry police detective who grilled him so mercilessly the other day. She had no umbrella to keep off the rain and to his harassed eye she resembled a drowned Yeti as she glared at him across the open grave.

The rest of the congregation consisted of a

handful of Kaitlyn's relatives who had turned up in a dilapidated people carrier having stopped off at the pub on the way here. He'd hardly spoken a word to them since their arrival. The woman called Linda, apparently Kaitlyn's mother, sneered down into the hole looking more annoyed than grief-stricken, and the others, Kaitlyn's siblings and her mother's latest partner, wasted no time in returning to their vehicle once the vicar had concluded his dirge-like monologue.

The police had located the family and passed on their contact information. From the brief exchange Luke had with Linda Byrne it was clear that they wouldn't have bothered to make the trip from Manchester had he not offered to pay for their petrol and put a substantial tab behind the bar at a local pub in lieu of an official wake.

He'd imagined that Kaitlyn would have wanted her family present for this occasion. Having met them he now suspected he'd been mistaken. It was something they'd never discussed. And why would they? Even with Luke's previous near-death experience their sheer youth gave them delusions of immortality. When he finally took the opportunity to open up about his fears with her, back on that terrible night, it wasn't with any sense of impending doom. He certainly never dreamed that Kaitlyn was in any danger.

He shuddered, whether from the cold or the dread which hovered constantly at his shoulder, he couldn't be sure.

By now Kaitlyn's family would be spending his money at the bar, the Scottish copper had finally dragged herself away and Luke and his mother were alone at the graveside. Her shivering rumbled through him and the weight of her hand on his arm was a plea to leave this miserable place. With a last kiss blown towards the mahogany casket Luke allowed himself to be drawn towards the waiting limousine.

*

The key was bulky and heavy, an unusual shape made for a custom-built lock. It would be virtually impossible to pick the lock that this key was designed to fit, even for a professional thief. The gloomy old house had been sealed, a crime scene, the key to the lock held in police possession. Despite the lack of a satisfactory conclusion to their enquires, the property had been released, the key returned to the owner, one Luke Kirkwood. But in the meantime Detective Sergeant Debbie McDougall had taken the opportunity to have a copy made. She'd had to call in a favour to get it done so accurately and so quickly. No high street locksmith had a key-cutter that could reproduce this while you wait.

She was only able to collect the key this morning. DI Penn insisted that she show her face at the funeral, soaking herself in the torrential downpour, ostensibly as a sign of respect but also to let the Kirkwood boy know he hadn't been forgotten, so this was the first chance she'd had to try it out.

Just pop it in the slot, give a twist to see if it works, then lock it up again and walk away. No unlawful entry.

Not today, at any rate.

They'd had to release the property far too soon for her liking. Forensics had given it the all-clear but there was something about the place that didn't feel right to DS McDougall. 'Unchancy' her ma would have said as she kissed the crucifix that hung permanently round her neck. In Debbie's more down to earth terminology she felt the place 'gied her the wullies'. But that was by far underplaying the aura of unease and foreboding that his house exuded.

Penn had laughed off her suggestion that there was something 'wrong' with the building, and any explanation she offered sounded weak and ridiculous.

'Hunches are out of date,' he'd said. 'You're living in the past. These days it's all about evidence and forensics. You can't just follow your nose anymore.'

Her ma had always claimed she had a 'witch's nose' and Debbie occasionally sensed things that others were unaware of. Maybe she'd inherited her mother's supernatural snout. Whatever the case, something about that boy and this house definitely smelled off.

Sweeping her unruly, rain-sodden hair from her face McDougall stepped up to the door and raised the key. Before she could even insert her shiny new prize into the lock the heavy portal swung smoothly open, its awful creak setting her teeth on edge.

But how could that be?

Had the forensics team failed to secure the place when they left? Surely not, they were notoriously fastidious. Perhaps Luke Kirkwood and his mother visited the house before attending the girl's funeral and in their grief-stricken state simply forgot to lock up after themselves. Not that Emma Kirkwood showed signs of being particularly stricken with grief.

They'd been holed up in their 'place in the country' since that tragic night when the girl had died in 'mysterious circumstances'.

'Mysterious, ma fanny!' McDougall had said at the time, wanting nothing more than to slam the cell door on Luke Kirkwood's scrawny arse and 'chuck the key oot the windae'. But the more time she spent in this house during the investigation the more convinced she'd become that something wasn't right.

'Hulloo!' she called, peering into the dim hallway. 'Is anybody thurr?'

The rich Rs of her thick accent rolled back at her from the darkness but no other sound greeted her, nor was there any sign of movement within the house.

She shouldn't be here. Just close the door and walk away, that was the sensible thing to do. The Kirkwoods might return at any time. She had no authority to enter the premises. But something was drawing her inside. It was as real to her as a gilt-edged card with 'You are cordially invited' printed on it in a fancy, flowing font.

McDougall stepped over the threshold, tense, alert, nerves on fire.

She ignored the downstairs rooms. Whatever wanted her here was up the stairs, along that dimly-illuminated corridor, lurking in the room at the far end. The room where Thomas Kirkwood died. The room where Kaitlyn Mondae died. It wasn't credible that anyone could be in there, but DS Debbie McDougall went to meet them anyway.

Luke Kirkwood was bawbag-deep in this, she had no doubt, but there was no way he could have returned to the house faster than her. If there was someone awaiting her up ahead, it wasn't him.

The study door stood ajar, enticing, beckoning. Only now, steps away from the portal, did her stride falter. Her skin tingled and a strange weight pressed on her chest. Was this what fear felt like? Hardened criminals twice her size never brought this weakness to her knees, this quiver to her hands.

Whispered voices reached her from within. Or maybe one voice, echoed, repeated, speaking over itself, breathy and sibilant.

'You can't have him.'

'Leave him be.'

'The boy is mine.'

McDougall inched a leg forward. Her heavy boot nudged the door. It swung wide with a sigh of oiled hinges.

'Who's thurr?' she called. 'This is the po-liss. Show yursell!'

The whispering ceased and the gloomy room showed no signs of occupancy.

'Ah hearrt ye,' she said. 'Ah ken ye're thurr. Come oot whurr ah can see ye.'

A curious sensation overwhelmed her as she moved into the chamber, as if she were pushing through heavy drapes and wading against an incoming tide, all at once. She shook away distracting mixed metaphors with a toss of her thick red hair, as ice cubes crawled along her spine on spiders' legs, and slowly took in her surroundings.

Shadows loomed around her, greedy, oppressive, and she reached for the light switch to dispel their power. But it wasn't where she remembered it to be. As part of the investigation team looking into Kaitlyn Mondae's sudden death she'd spent enough time here to become familiar with the layout of the place, but even in this dim light she could tell that things were subtly changed.

She took out her mobile and tapped the torch app. Jagged shapes lurched around her, leaping amongst the furnishings. In the swooping beam the *chaise longue* seemed newer, less shabby, and the big wing chair looked to be a slightly different design. Had the Kirkwoods attempted to erase unhappy memories by redecorating?

An insistent tick-tock impinged on her awareness and her torch fell upon a large grandfather clock standing tall and proud in the corner. That hadn't been there the last time she was here. Its ornate minute hand lingered just shy of the twelve, where the shorter hand already sat, awaiting its companion.

Mid-day? The mechanism must be running slow. Kaitlyn's funeral was at 11.30 this morning and that ended over an hour ago. McDougall attempted to activate her phone's screen to check the time but it remained blank and, as she watched, the torch beam faded to nothing, leaving the room in pitch black, darker even than when she entered. She'd charged the phone in the car on the way here. Damn thing must be faulty.

No light flooded in as she whisked the curtains wide, the sky beyond the pane much darker than storm clouds might bring. This was middle-of-the-night darkness, mixed with a heavy fog that hadn't been there moments earlier, before she came into this building.

The only illumination out there came from the streetlight on the corner, but its pale glow was inconsistent, flickering, as if it was a gas-powered flame rather than the hard-wired electric bulb she knew it must be.

The ticking echoed louder as the minute hand crept closer to the hour.

McDougall recalled the phrase her boss, DI Penn, was so fond of teasing her with. 'You're living in the past, Debbie.'

Then the clock struck midnight and, as the last chime faded, the room stood silent, cold and empty.

Chapter Seventeen

'You could have gone with them.'

'What?'

'To the pub. Had a drink.'

Luke stared at his mother as if her suggestion were the most absurd thing he had ever heard.

'And talk about what?' he grumbled. 'The weather? The economy? How much we have in common?'

'Just to be sociable.'

Emma shrugged, helpless, clearly at a loss when dealing with grief amongst the lower classes. Luke's father's funeral had been a lavish affair, attended by hundreds, Rolls-Royces and Bentleys queueing along the narrow lanes criss-crossing the cemetery, not an MPV in sight.

No police officers in sight, either.

'Just to show your face for five minutes,' Emma continued. 'I'd have been fine.'

'They'll not miss me.'

Luke stripped off his black tie and hurled it into a chair. Emma picked it up and coiled it carefully around her hand.

'Then we should've gone straight home, instead of coming back here. Another couple of hours and we'd have been in our own place.'

Pressure was gradually building behind Luke's eyes and he held cold fingers against his forehead to stave off the impending migraine.

They stood in the kitchen of the house in town, coats and jackets hanging in the hall, umbrella draining in the sink. Luke leaned past it to run the cold tap for a moment, then filled a glass with water.

'This is my own place,' he said.

'Well, yes, technically, but—'

Luke cut her off.

'I have to be here.'

'What?'

'Here,' he repeated. 'I have to be here.'

'Why?'

He hesitated, unsure of his answer.

'Because... I don't know. It's just... I do, that's all.'

The cupboards were bare and they had few belongings in the house, but when the driver asked where they wished to be taken Luke immediately gave him this address.

'You're just being silly.' Emma dipped into her handbag and retrieved her phone.

'It's not too late. I'll get the car back and we can—'

'I want to be here,' Luke insisted.

She was still scrolling her contacts. Luke took the phone from her hand and dropped it back into her bag.

She sighed.

'I know you're upset.'

'Upset?'

'Of course you are, it's been a terrible—'

'Upset doesn't come anywhere near how I'm feeling!'

He closed his eyes and saw her there. Kaitlyn. Spinning and swaying, gliding naked across the room, feet scuffing on the bare boards. Moving to music only she could hear. Pale skin glowing in the dim light.

'She died right there in front of me.'

Pain throbbed in his temples and he heard her last breath once more, forming his name.

For the millionth time since that night he cradled her against him as the spark faded in her pretty eyes.

'Dancing, like a maniac. Until she died!'

'Luke, don't...'

He shook off her soothing hand.

'And you think I'm merely upset?'

'It wasn't your fault,' Emma said. Her hands fluttered at her sides. She wanted so desperately to wrap him in her arms but knew he wouldn't allow it in his present disposition.

'Why couldn't I stop her?'

'We don't know what she'd taken.'

To her it was the obvious explanation. The only explanation.

Luke turned to her, fury in his gaze.

'Fuck you!'

She stepped back from his temper.

'Luke!'

'She had the occasional bit of weed, nothing stronger.'

His anger was partially aimed inward, for the notion had occurred to him, too. But he knew they'd checked her blood and found nothing. The angry cop had told him that much – used it as evidence of his guilt.

'No one blames you.'

A tear spilled from his eyes, left a damp trail down his shirt front.

'I do.'

She fought his resistance, held him against her.

'I think...' He choked on his words, forced them out. 'I think I loved her.'

Emma stroked his hair.

'No, you didn't.'

He pushed her away.

'What?!'

Her words were calm, reasonable.

'You were fond of her, you watched her die, now you feel guilty. Don't pretend it was more than that.'

'God, you can be such a cow, sometimes.'

Emma turned her back to him, to hide the pain in her eyes.

'I have to be strong, for you. What state would you be in if I allowed you to wallow in self-pity?'

'There's strong, and then there's callous.'

When she turned back her eyes were dry, her gaze steady.

'It's a fine line.'

She took the water from him, poured it down the sink.

'Have a proper drink,' she said. 'Your father kept some brandy in the study.'

'I'm not going up there.'

'I'll get it.'

She headed for the hallway.

'It'll make you feel better.'

'Will it?'

'Let's see, shall we?'

She slipped from the kitchen, heels clicking on the stairs and along the upper corridor. Luke listened, intent, breath caught in his chest. Listened – for what? A scream? Sounds of conflict? The thump of a body falling to the floor?

Within a moment Emma's footsteps returned down the stairs and Luke breathed again.

'Here we are,' she said, brandishing the decanter.

She poured two glasses, passed one to Luke.

He took it without response but placed it untouched on the table.

Emma sighed.

'You must make an effort, darling.'

'To do what?'

'To pull yourself together.'

'Am I coming apart?'

She stroked his cheek.

'A little, yes.'

With a roll of his eyes he hoisted the glass in a toast gesture and knocked back the contents in one.

'Better?' he asked.

'I should ask you that question.'

'It'll take more than one.'

'Well, then...'

She took back the glass and refilled it.

'How will getting completely rat-arsed help me to pull myself together?'

She closed her hand over his as she passed back the glass.

'It will disguise where you're coming apart.'

He took it a little slower this time but soon passed the glass back to be replenished again.

'We'll take a few minutes to warm ourselves through,' Emma said, handing him the fresh drink, 'then head back to the big house.'

'I told you, I'm staying here. You can go if you want to.'

'Don't worry, I'll drive.'

'You're not listening.'

'You've not said anything worth listening to.'

A tetchiness crept back into her voice.

'You want to stay in this mausoleum but you can't tell me why.'

Luke swirled the golden liquid in his glass, watched the light dancing in the ripples.

'He wants me here.'

'Who does?'

He held his silence for a long moment, until

he saw her take a breath to repeat her question.

'Mister Nice,' he said.

'Mister Nice?'

There was humour in her voice, as if she thought he was kidding, but the grim set of his features caught the laugh in her throat.

'Your nightmare man?' she asked, memories of wet beds and midnight cuddles returning. 'I thought you shook him off when you were ten.'

'He's back,' Luke said. 'He's real. And he's here.'

'Perhaps the drinks weren't such a good idea.'

She reached for his glass but he deflected her hand with his free hand, downed the brandy, then passed her the empty glass.

She placed it by the decanter but made no move to refill it this time.

'All this has hit you hard, darling,' she said. 'First your father, then your friend.'

Luke snarled his frustration.

'She had a name, Mother!'

'Yes, yes, Kaitlyn. I'm sorry.'

She slipped her arm though his, as she had by the graveside.

'This place isn't helping your frame of mind,' she said. 'Why don't we—?'

Luke pulled free from her grip.

'No!'

'All right, all right, we'll wait until you... feel better.'

He gave her a hard look then pushed past her to reach the decanter.

'I really don't think you ought to—'

The doorbell rang, freezing them both where they stood.

Who could be here? They weren't expecting anyone. Kaitlyn's family didn't have this address.

'Perhaps you could get that?' Luke said, lifting the decanter.

'Are you sure?' Emma asked. 'You don't seem in the mood for visitors.'

'I'm fine.'

The impasse lingered, neither moving, neither blinking, until the doorbell rang again.

Emma strode from the room.

Luke poured another drink, listening to the voices from the hall.

Emma returned in the company of a curious little man in tweeds and round-rimmed spectacles, dripping with rain. She relieved him of the sodden newspaper he'd been using as an umbrella and helped him peel off the jacket which clung to him with damp, an exercise which required much swapping of hands on the briefcase he nursed so carefully.

'This is Mr Phillips,' Emma said.

Howard wiped a wet hand on his shirt and extended it out towards Luke.

'Howard.'

Luke nodded and took another sip of his brandy.

'He claims he was a friend of your father,' Emma continued, disbelief heavy in her voice.

'Well, acquaintance,' Howard admitted. 'I only really met him the once.'

'Nice to meet you, I'm sure,' Luke drawled, raising his glass. 'Drink?'

Howard's face widened in horror. 'Oh, no, no, no!' he said, glasses almost slipping from his nose as he shook his head. 'Just a small one.'

Luke laughed and searched the cupboards for another glass.

'How did you know my husband, Mr Phillips?' Emma asked, frost still lingering in her tone.

'Could I persuade you to call me H.P.?'

'Not easily.'

'Oh.'

Howard took the drink that Luke held out to him, grimacing as he took a sip.

'Your husband sought me out, Mrs Kirkwood, to assist him on a particular project.'

'Really?'

Knocking back the rest of the brandy Howard puffed out his chest and said, proudly, 'Because of my specialist knowledge.'

'And what is your field, Mr Phillips?'

The man hesitated, and Luke noticed a redness creeping up from the collar of his shirt and spotting his round cheeks. Was he embarrassed, or was it merely the warmth of the house after the dreadful weather outside? Or was the brandy getting to him already?

'Actually,' Howard began, looking from one to the other of them, 'I'm an occult investigator.'

Emma's mouth dropped open and Luke wondered if he himself was a victim of too many drinks. Had their visitor just said what he thought he said?

'You're a ghost buster?' he asked, incredulous.

Howard raised a defensive hand. 'Well, no, that's a bit—'

'A demon hunter?'

The red splodge had spread across Howard's features.

'I wouldn't put it in such simple terms.'

Luke couldn't resist teasing the man.

'Howard Phillips?' he asked. 'Shouldn't a demon buster have a cool, impressive name, Like John Constantine or Harry Dresden?'

Howard looked puzzled.

'I'm afraid I don't know—'

'Or Skulduggery Pleasant?'

Having exhausted his supply of literary spooky detectives Luke poised the decanter over Howard's glass.

'I really shouldn't,' Howard said, holding the glass steady for him.

Luke made it a generous measure.

'As a matter of fact,' Howard continued, 'there's an amusing coincidence regarding my name, you see—'

Emma cut off the anecdote with a raised hand.

'I'm sure there is,' she said. 'Perhaps you could tell us why my husband... sought you out?'

'Yes, yes, of course, forgive my deviation!'

Flustered, Howard lifted the briefcase and pointed to the kitchen table.

'May I?'

'Please,' said Emma, moving a chair from his path.

Luke marvelled at her composure, though it was clear that her patience was straining.

Howard seemed oblivious as he fumbled with the bag, wrestling with the catch.

'I was sorry to hear about the death of your husband.'

'So was I,' Emma said.

'Er, quite.'

Howard wet his dry mouth with another sip of brandy.

'It seems,' he began, 'that your husband had some concerns about something which occurred in this building some time ago. In the room upstairs, to be more precise.'

'Something occurred?'

'My apologies.'

Howard hung his head, chastened.

'I'm guilty of the very vagueness that I'm usually so critical of. It would appear, from the evidence collected by your late husband, that this residence was the location of a visitation, or perhaps more correctly, a manifestation of an infernal nature.'

Luke chuckled. The strange little man amused him. It was just what he needed on a day like today.

'And this is you not being vague, is it?' he said.

'I don't understand a word he's saying.' Emma directed her words past Howard as if he were a waiter in a Spanish restaurant.

'Apparently the devil was here.'

'Not the devil as such,' Howard said. 'If only that were the case.'

'I'm sorry,' Luke said, 'are you saying that having the devil in the house would be a good thing?'

'Yes,' Howard replied, then reconsidered. 'Well, no, obviously not, but, yes, in a way.'

He noticed their perplexed expressions.

'You see,' he clarified, 'where creatures of the nether world are concerned, having knowledge of that being's name is a massive advantage. It gives one power over that being. Conjurings and invocations are greatly simplified.'

Luke felt that there was more to come.

'And...?'

'Well, the devil himself has so many names. Satan and Lucifer being the most obvious, but there's also Beelzebub, Diabolus, Baphomet, Moloch, Tezcatlipoka...'

Howard took such relish over that last name

that Luke felt he should stop him there.

'Right, right, but none of them were the one you're talking about?'

Howard wagged a finger at Luke's schoolboy error.

'As I say, it's not "them", those are all names for the singular entity that people refer to as—'

'But not him,' Luke interjected, before Howard could begin another lengthy explanation.

'Er, no,' Howard conceded. 'Not him.'

Howard reached into the briefcase, pulled out the ancient tome which Thomas Kirkwood had discovered amongst his ancestor's possessions. He placed it on the table, hands hovering above it, as if afraid prolonged contact might burn him.

'I believe we are dealing with a lesser demon of some sort.'

He spotted the glance that Luke and his mother shared, and mistook their amusement for complacency.

'But no less dangerous, for all that,' he warned. 'There are a number of categories of demon that might apply here. A djinn, perhaps.'

Emma's bewilderment was growing.

'Gin?'

'A djinn,' Howard corrected, rolling the word around his teeth. 'Root of the popular fantasy of the genie. Usually ephemeral in nature, but in many circumstances they are able to interact with humans in a physical way. Also incubi and succubi—'

'Oh, I've heard of them,' Luke interjected eagerly, recalling reading something in a teenage fantasy novel. 'They're the sex ones, right?'

'Sex ones?' said Emma, aghast.

The colour was returning to Howard's jowls.

'Um, yes,' he mumbled. 'Those creatures are

known to consort with people on a carnal level, in their attempt to exert an influence over them.'

Emma rolled her eyes.

'And probably all the more successful because of it,' she said.

'Well,' Howard conceded, 'there are many tales—'

Luke couldn't resist a lascivious snigger.

'I bet there are!'

Howard began to slide the book back into the briefcase.

'Your father was far more willing to take this seriously,' he said. 'I'd imagined you would be interested in what he was looking into.'

They'd offended him. Luke felt a pang of regret, the man was so intent and serious his bumbling came across as pompous. Luke tried to keep the amusement from his voice but even he could tell he'd failed.

'I'm sorry, Mr Phillips.'

Howard ignored the insincere remark.

'Especially,' he began, importantly, 'as it may have been directly responsible for his death.'

Luke was stunned and his mother's face dropped in astonishment.

'I beg your pardon!?' she gasped.

'But clearly,' Howard went on, his pride severely dented, 'this is all merely a joke to you, therefore I'll bid you good day.'

Luke placed a hand on the briefcase, halting Howard's retreat.

'Whoa, wait! How can this have anything to do with my father's death?'

'My husband had a heart attack,' Emma said, coolly. 'Natural causes.'

Howard looked at her, hesitated, pondered his next words.

'Had he suffered extensively with cardiac issues prior to the night of his death?'

Emma grudgingly shook her head.

'Well, no, I can't say that he had. But the post mortem was quite conclusive.'

Howard nodded, though his face betrayed his misgivings.

'I'm sure it was.'

He held up his hands in submission.

'It isn't my intention to cause you any further distress, Mrs Kirkwood. I'll say no more.'

'Oh, no no no,' Luke said. 'You'll say plenty more, Mr Phillips.'

Howard looked at Luke's hand on the briefcase. It was clear he wasn't going to move it. Luke and Emma regarded him keenly.

'I had intended to keep my suspicions to myself, after Thomas – Mr Kirkwood – passed away. But in light of the more recent occurrence...'

'What occurrence?' Emma snapped, bewildered by the strange visitor's utterings.

Luke sighed heavily and shook his head.

'Kaitlyn!' he reminded her.

She nodded and mouthed an apology.

'Two unexpected deaths within a few months,' Howard said. 'Both taking place at a point of supernatural significance. Not something I can easily ignore. Hence my return today.'

Pulling a chair from beneath the table Luke slumped onto the seat. The man's words were incomprehensible, but if he could make sense of the crazy goings on here then Luke was willing to listen. He could see no connection between his father's death and that of Kaitlyn, beyond the location, but Howard claimed a link existed. A tremor ran through him as he began to suspect what that link may be.

Luke forced himself to concentrate on the soft voice as Howard continued.

'The visitation that your husband was investigating took place many, many years ago, but I fear that some being, some malevolent power, may be present in this house, even now. Either summoned inadvertently by Thomas himself during his explorations into the occult, or dormant for over a hundred years and just recently reanimated.'

Silence fell over the room as Howard allowed his words to penetrate.

Fingernails scraping the table top, Luke's sibilant whisper could barely be heard.

'It's Mister Nice.'

Howard leaned closer, head cocked.

'Come again?'

Moving round to stand by her son Emma squeezed his shoulder.

'Luke, darling.'

It felt like an admonishment or warning. Luke shook off the hand.

'It is. It's him.'

'Who?' asked Howard. This latest exchange had left him befuddled.

'Mister Nice,' Luke repeated. 'I know it sounds funny, but—'

'No, no, on the contrary,' Howard cut in. 'It sounds bloody creepy, if I may be forgiven. Urgh! Mister Nice.'

He shuddered, theatrically.

'He's a throwback to my childhood nightmares.'

Howard nodded deeply, as if this made perfect sense.

'Nightmares are a common access point for

demonic ingress or possession. They give the intruder power but are readily dismissed in the daylight, so we blame a film we saw, or that piece of cheese we ate too late in the evening.'

Howard was already lifting the briefcase.

'I don't think Mister Nice is a name we'll find in here, but he might have a connection with one of the known demons.'

He gestured towards the house beyond the confines of the kitchen.

'Might we retire to the study?' he asked. 'That would seem to be the focus of the incursion.'

'The study?'

Luke hadn't returned to that ill-fated room since the night of Kaitlyn's death. His face paled at the prospect of entering the chamber again.

Emma recognised his reticence, leaned in to stroke his tightly clenched hand.

'That's not a good idea,' she said. 'Can't you do whatever you need to do down here?'

Howard's eyes flitted round the fitments.

'In the kitchen?'

Luke placed his free hand over Emma's, grateful for her concern.

'I'll be fine,' he said. 'It's time I faced the place again.'

He led the way up the stairs, though his progress faltered on the upper corridor.

'Luke,' said Emma, 'you don't have to—'

'I do.'

With a deep breath he stepped over the threshold, nerves jangling as he stared at the spot where Kaitlyn had lain, limp and unresponsive after dancing so insanely. He expected... what? The ceiling to cave in upon them? The walls to come crashing down, crushing them in the rubble?

Instead?

Nothing.

The dull grey light of the miserable afternoon seeped through the windows. The room felt melancholy but not dangerous. Sad, but not sadistic.

He was almost disappointed. None of the horror of his last visit lingered in the atmosphere. How dare it be so ordinary?

Howard bustled past him, setting the briefcase down onto the desk.

He began to unbutton his sleeve cuffs.

'Do you mind if I make myself comfortable?'

The notion of being comfortable in this room seemed inconceivable to Luke. He gave an awkward laugh.

'Not at all.'

Sleeves rolled up, Howard bent to the task of examining the book once more.

Chapter Eighteen

The book slipping from her hand woke Emma from a doze. She took a moment to try to find the page she had been reading, then gave up and tossed the book onto the bed. She hadn't been concentrating on it anyway, couldn't even recall the plot. Some flimsy historical romance. Trivial, banal. Paragraphs had floated before her eyes, content and meaning lost as her mind meandered elsewhere. Drifting back to the study, and their unexpected guest.

Could there be any veracity to that strange little man's claims? It was true that Thomas had become obsessed with this place and those journals he'd discovered, but it was hard to imagine that the scrawling in those yellowed pages was anything other than insane ramblings.

Demons? Visitations? Nonsense!

But Thomas was the one who invited that – what did he call himself? – occult investigator here to make sense of what he had read. Was Howard Phillips a charlatan, taking advantage of her husband's desperation for answers? No other explanation was conceivable. But she would never have described Thomas as a gullible man.

She cocked her head, listened intently. No voices carried along the corridor from the study. The time on her phone, propped up on the bedside table like an alarm clock, told her she must have slept longer than she realised. Two hours had passed since she finally despaired of the supernatural mumbo jumbo being bandied about and left Luke and Phillips to it, retiring to her room and her bed.

Perhaps she shouldn't have left Luke with their mysterious visitor. Shock and grief had made him vulnerable. He'd had no time to recover from his father's death before this latest incident with that girl and, for all his bluster and bravado, Emma knew that the accident last year affected him deeply, even now. And why was he dredging up childhood nightmares after more than ten years?

Mister Nice.

The name he would scream in his sleep, night after night, waking in tears, sheets soaked with sweat and urine. Surely he left that trauma behind, an infantile myth such as Santa Claus or the Tooth Fairy. This place, those books, all those gruesome skulls and statuettes and weird, horrible objects were no good for a sensitive boy like him to have surrounding him. They needed to go. If he wouldn't allow the cleaners to dispose of them then there was nothing else for it, she would have to do it herself. Now, while he slept, she could collect them all up and throw them in the bin. He'd be angry, no doubt, but presented with a fait accompli he would have no choice but to accept her decision and return to Surrey with her in the morning.

They would lock this place up and not look back. The lawyers would be set on looking for a loophole in the terms of his father's will, or, failing that, the house could stand abandoned, gathering dust and market value until Luke reached twenty-five.

It seemed such a good idea, back when Thomas first proposed it – locking Luke into possession of the building, teaching him about property and investment. At the time the suggestion that Thomas might actually die before Luke far exceeded that age was ludicrous, no more than a legal technicality, the will itself a formality his lawyers had insisted upon.

None of them had the merest inkling of how events would transpire. Thomas dying right here, followed by Luke's dancer friend, that Phillips person turning up and all this ghoulish talk, hinting that Thomas's death might be other than natural causes.

She had a responsibility to put an end to this madness right now. She slipped a long dressing gown over her silk nightdress and steeled herself for what she must do. She had no desire to touch a single one of the journals or artefacts but she could see no alternative.

The corridor was dark, forbidding. Luke's bedroom door was closed but at the opposite end of the hall the study door stood ajar and a faint light spilled out. Had Luke left on the desk lamp by mistake when he went to bed, or was he in there still, poring over those dreadful books?

As she crept closer indistinct voices reached her. He was in there. But who could he be talking to at this hour?

'Still up?' she asked, stepping into the room.

There was no one else there after all. Luke sat alone in the pool of light from the lamp, hunched over the desk. He wore a long housecoat over his pyjamas. She assumed he had gone to bed, lain restless and disturbed, and been drawn back to this eerie place.

'Yes,' he said. 'We both are.'

'Both?'

She glanced around, checking the shadows. Was that a figure sitting in the large, wing-backed chair? She flicked on the main switch. The chandelier's bulbs struggled to reach the far corners but enough light was raised to show that the chamber was empty but for the two of them.

'Yorick and I were just having a little *tete-a-tete.*'

One of the horrible skulls sat on the desktop before him. He peered into its deep, empty sockets, as if communing with the long-absent spirit who once resided within.

Emma shivered at the image.

She sauntered over to the drinks cabinet, as if she had no other reason for being there. The brandy decanter still stood on the kitchen table, so she selected the whisky and poured two glasses.

'I take it your father's strange friend has gone?'

Luke stretched in the chair, cracked his neck.

'Howard? Yes, scuttled off back to his coven, bless him.'

'Good.'

She placed a tumbler of whisky on the desk beside the skull. Luke stared at it but didn't touch it.

'Don't be unkind, Mother.'

'Don't tell me you like the creepy little man?'

Luke swivelled in the chair so that he was looking at her.

'If he and Dad were "bezzies" then that's recommendation enough for me.'

'Acquaintances,' she corrected. 'He said as much himself.'

He shrugged, spun the chair in a complete circle until he was facing her again. Now the skull was in his lap, tilted to stare up at her.

She turned away, sipped her drink.

'Did he succeed in exorcising the place?'

Luke rose and returned 'Yorick' to his place on the shelf.

'If I thought that was a serious question then I might discuss it with you.'

'I'm deadly serious. If a man like your father could give credence to all this, then who am I to disregard it?'

'Did he never talk to you about it?'

'Not it any great detail, but I was aware his interests had taken a... dark turn.'

She recalled the evening by the pool back home. His talk of death and what lies beyond.

She refilled her glass, took a deep mouthful.

'I miss him so very much.'

'Do you?'

'Of course.'

'You rarely speak of him.'

'I think of him often.'

He leaned in close, placed a tender kiss on the top of her head.

She stroked his cheek.

'Thank goodness I still have you,' she said.

'You'll always have me,' he promised. 'I'm going nowhere.'

'Bold words, from the boy who diced with death a year ago.'

'I've told you,' he laughed, 'I'm indestructible.'

She rested her hand on his chest, felt the steady thumping within.

'So your father thought, until his heart betrayed him.'

Luke's face grew dark and pensive.

'If it was his heart.'

'What else? Your Mister Nice?'

'Maybe.'

He picked up the drink from the desk, swirled

it around the glass.

'Or whatever thing is lurking here.'

Around them the shadows seemed to be waging a war against the light, gaining ground little by little.

'Then why do you insist on staying here?'

'It won't let me go.'

Tears formed in the corners of his haunted eyes.

A notion insinuated itself into her mind, no fragmentary hint or idea, but a fully-formed certainty.

'It's hungry,' she said.

'What?'

'This place, or the thing inhabiting it.'

'Hungry?'

She felt it now, whatever was troubling him, the presence, the essence in the walls around them, as a physical force lurking in the encroaching gloom.

'Greedy. A huge, lustful appetite that hasn't been sated.'

She pressed herself against him, body cold and rigid.

He held her, felt her trembling.

'Mum?'

'It's taken your father, and that girl, but it hasn't finished. It wants more!'

The words tumbled from her, unbidden, unrehearsed.

'Don't let it take me, too!'

'I won't.'

She grasped the lapels of his robe in her clenched fists, eyes wild.

'Promise me, Luke!'

'I promise! I'll keep you safe.'

'Safe? Can you?'

Something was with them, unseen, unheard. Would they ever be safe again?

'Of course. I can and I will'

The comfort in his embrace was fading, as if he were pulling away from her, though he stood as close as before. She clutched tighter at his gown, pulled him down to her, so she could nestle her face against his.

'Don't worry,' he whispered, lips close to her ear.

'Don't worry,' she echoed.

This was what she needed. Her protector, her guardian. His arms around her, his warmth on this cold night. She tilted her head, moved her mouth over his, warm, needful.

Hungry.

He pulled away, tore his lips from hers.

'Mum? What the hell...?'

Her hands still clawed at him.

'Your father. That slut. They're gone now.'

Her words, her thoughts, were new, fresh, real and urgent.

'We don't need them, as long as we've got each other!'

'What are you talking about?'

Why couldn't he see what she saw, understand the need, the hunger?

The desire.

She threw off her robe, ran her hands over her body. Felt the silk of her nightgown, smooth and sensuous on her skin.

'Come here, my darling boy.'

He shook his head, aghast.

'Stop this, please!'

He seized her clutching hands, holding them from him. She reversed the motion, drew his hands to her, her flesh cold under the burning fire of his caress.

'Hold me, touch me!'

He snatched his hands away.

'No!'

As she launched herself at him again he swiped a slap across her face, sharp and hard.

She dropped to the floor, limp, heavy.

'What the hell's come over you?'

He backed away, horrified.

Her mind awhirl, she tried to make sense of the last few moments. Those words, those actions! It was her, but not her. Like watching a marionette wearing her face, guided by another's hand.

'I didn't... That wasn't...'

She struggled to translate her muddled thoughts into coherent words.

'You're shaken, upset,' he said, forceful, strong, the adult now to her naughty child.

She reached out to him, but he stepped away.

'You've been drinking,' he continued, and she trembled at the distaste in his voice. 'Go to bed. Sleep it off.'

He strode to the door. The expression on his face as he paused and turned back to her held a mixture of sorrow and disgust.

'We'll talk in the morning.'

And he was gone.

Lying there, alone, as the sound of his slippers on the hall floor receded into the distance, she listened to the silence crowding around her. But it wasn't total quiet she heard. Someone was laughing. Here, in the room with her. A malevolent chuckle, a guttural rumble that rolled from wall to wall and echoed inside her head.

No one.

But the shadows were closer. Were the overhead bulbs failing?

She slowly dragged herself to her feet. The weird experience of a moment ago had left her dizzy, disorientated. Hands outstretched for balance she was drawn to the large chair by the fireplace. The Chesterfield swallowed her into its embrace as she surrendered to the pull.

Her eyes closed, her mind swam, until she wasn't sure if she was awake or lost in dream. That couldn't be a real hand, its icy fingers stroking her arm, her shoulder, her breast. She surely imagined that mouth, hot and wet, nuzzling her neck, her face, her lips.

Forcing open her eyelids she stared directly into horror! Something – a man, something else? – leaned over her, its revolting features so close they blurred in her vision. A face from horror movies, every monster ever imagined, crushed and pulped into one hideous form.

Kissing her! Tongue, dry and rough, writhing, insinuating itself into her mouth.

Was this the creature from Luke's nightmares come alive? Childhood terror hiding in the shadows, a dream no longer? Scornful rejection wasn't an option, as it had been when she had changed an eight-year-old boy's wet pyjamas, or taken the arm of a grief-stricken young man fresh from his lover's funeral. The time for denial had passed. He was here.

Mister Nice.

She tried to move, push him from her, but his weight held her trapped. She tried to scream, call for help, but his mouth stilled her voice and stole her breath. He ignored her clawing fingernails, her thrashing fists. Tears clouded her vision and her heart pounded in her chest.

Nothing existed but those bloodshot eyes glaring unblinking into her own.

The darkness from the corners of the room came surging towards her like a relentless tide and all she knew was the gentle embrace of Mister Nice, and the tender kiss of death.

Book Four

Howard Phillips

Chapter Nineteen

'Weirdo.'

'Freak.'

'Nutter.'

Children can be cruel.

Howard Phillips had recognised his gift at an early age. His mistake had been to tell people about it. Describing the things he saw and felt had brought derision and ridicule from others in the schools and homes into which he was placed. Foster carers found it difficult to become close to him. Mention of spiritual or otherworldly things prompted uncomfortable silences at the dinner table. Telling someone that a recently deceased relative was watching them from the corner of the room was often less reassuring than he had intended it to be.

Most people, adult or child, dismissed his abilities outright. Any who didn't would shun him or avoid him. In the worst cases they might attribute the sudden death of his parents in a road accident when he was eight, which he alone survived, to dark forces conjured up by the mysterious young boy.

But he knew his mother and father did not hold him accountable, for they had told him so on numerous occasions since their deaths.

Struggling to find someone with whom he could converse who didn't reside in an alternative dimension or plane of existence did little to develop his social skills, but it did allow him plenty of time to concentrate on his study of the arcane arts and practices which was his sole interest. Not for him the distractions of television, alcohol, girls. A single minded determination to master a field not covered in mainstream schools and universities took him to the darkened halls of obscure establishments in Oxford, Edinburgh and even as far afield as Arkham in Massachusetts.

All the intervening years, and all the wonders and horrors he had witnessed in that time, had finally led him back to this house yet again. The cold house. The unempty house. This third visit would be the last, of that he felt certain. He was determined to see an end to these diabolical shenanigans, once and for all.

As he pressed the doorbell Howard recalled his first time of calling here. Thomas Kirkwood's tentative welcome, initially dubious, his reservations gradually breaking down until, on the verge of leaving, he had heard the words which had touched him so deeply. It was just after Howard sensed the ominous chill in Thomas's study, following Howard's slipping of the ancient book, whose contents they had spent the previous hours pondering, into his battered satchel. A draught, Thomas supposed. Howard, less certain, kept his doubts to himself. Had he spoken up in that moment then the events which followed might not have transpired and Thomas might have lived to open the curtains and allow in the morning sun. Howard cursed himself for his reticence, felt he should have foreseen the consequences of separating the book from the house.

But all such thought swept deliriously from Howard's mind upon Thomas's response to his words of farewell.

Thomas held out a hand and said simply,

'Goodnight, H.P.'

Howard stood dumbfounded.

'You called me H.P.'

Thomas's grin broadened.

'I think you've earned it, don't you?'

Howard stared at Thomas's extended hand for long seconds, then slipped past it, moved in close and wrapped Thomas in a tight embrace.

Thomas looked at the smaller man in startled surprise, then chuckled and patted Howard warmly on the back.

Eyes averted, cheeks aglow, Howard released his host and mumbled an apology for his presumptuousness.

'Actually,' he said, to cover his embarrassment, 'there's an interesting story behind my nickname. It's—'

'Lovecraft,' Thomas interrupted with a knowing smile. 'Chronicler of numerous stories of dark, gothic fantasy and horror.'

He slipped his hands in his pockets and grinned in amusement as Howard gaped at him.

'Though many claim,' he went on, 'that Lovecraft merely repeated tales whispered to him by unknown voices, rather than imagining them himself.'

Howard's jaw still hung open.

'What... But...' he stammered. 'Why, that's—'

'H.P. Lovecraft,' Thomas said. 'Howard Phillips Lovecraft. I'm not completely illiterate, you know.'

Howard's gasp caught in his throat and he had to remind himself to keep breathing. No one had ever made the connection before. Whenever he mentioned in conversation the coincidence that an occult investigator should bear a name so similar to that of a famous writer of occult tales his listeners would shrug and move on, or completely ignore the reference. When Howard himself had discovered it his heart had swollen with pride and he'd taken it as a sign that his life was following the correct track – a predestined path set out for him by the ancient powers which governed all our fates.

That Thomas should pick up on it so quickly and astutely told him that their meeting was part of some deeper plan and their friendship was meant to be. Howard's eyes prickled as he turned to retrieve his bag.

'Are you crying, H.P.?'

Howard sniffed and cleared his throat.

'Of course not.'

'Good,' Thomas said, a hand on his shoulder, steering him to the door. 'We've got serious work to do tomorrow. No time for tears.'

Thomas had seen him out of the house, then returned to the study and faced his doom.

On his return the following evening Howard was unable to raise a response. It was a further two days before news reached him of Thomas's death. Surely that must call an end to the investigation? Thomas's search for truth was over and the Book of Shadows was safely in Howard's possession.

But the house still exuded a sinister aura and Howard made up his mind to keep it under close observation.

When a second death occurred Howard knew he must call again and make himself known to Thomas's wife and son, despite their almost certain resistance to his warnings. He was alarmed to discover that the newest resident of the house was haunted by a demonic stalker of his own. His Mister Nice, tormenting the lad while he slept. Taking a little boy's disturbed dreams and corrupting them into a young man's waking nightmare.

Luke Kirkwood reluctantly disclosed more of his anxiety – how his recent nightmares began after a near-death experience; the horror of his incapacitation while he witnessed his girlfriend's macabre dance of death.

Emma, his mother, remained disinclined to accept this talk of unworldly things and retired to her bed, leaving them in no doubt as to her distaste of the subject. Without the distraction of her harsh cynicism the conversation flowed more freely, though Luke failed to fully abandon his sceptical reserve.

By right of inheritance the Magoralian Text which Howard held so close was technically the property of Luke or his mother. Was keeping the book from them a form of theft? Thomas merely loaned it to him, with every intention of taking it back when their business resumed. Howard eased his guilt by persuading himself that he was a worthier custodian of what was essentially a dangerous artefact and his misdemeanour was perpetrated for their safety.

As their discussion drew to a conclusion Howard promised to consider what Luke had told him, with the aim of ridding the lad of his persecutor. He vowed his studies would take no more than a few days and promised to return with an answer as soon as was humanly possible. The glib rejoinder, 'Or as soon as is inhumanly possible,' took fractionally too long to form in his mind and comedic timing suggested that the moment was lost. On reflection he decided that was probably a good thing.

Having specified a few days as his target,

Howard was surprised to receive a call from Luke, sounding breathless and agitated, early the next morning, imploring Howard to return immediately, though without explanation of the sudden urgency.

'Bring your kit,' Luke had demanded.

'Kit?'

'Your exorcist shizzle,' the young man snapped. 'Crosses, holy water, puke-resistant overalls. I've not watched the film but I've seen the memes.'

Howard's frown must have travelled through the phone network, for Luke took a breath and softened his tone.

'Sorry. Come today. Soon as you can. Please.'

It was the *please* that swung it.

And so here he was, ringing the incongruously modern doorbell for the third and, he prayed to whatever gods might be listening, final time.

Darkness was closing in. Howard's efforts to prepare for the upcoming confrontation had been hastily completed, but he could not allow himself to be rushed too much. Therein would assuredly lie disaster.

Luke's impatience was evident as he dragged open the creaking door and beckoned Howard inside.

'It's getting late. I was beginning to think you weren't coming.'

He left Howard to close the door and led the way upstairs, the older man scurrying in his wake as Luke strode without any discernible hesitation into the study, the site of so much pain and misery.

'These things are always best conducted at night.'

Howard bumped the chunky, pilot-style case

he hefted along at his side against the edge of the door, mumbling an apology for his clumsiness.

Luke ignored the distraction.

'These things?'

'Any attempt to communicate with eldritch beings,' Howard explained.

'Eldritch?'

Luke's eyebrow twitched.

'Nice word. Like a good lie-in, do they, these eldritch beings?'

'Sunlight can deter the free movement of any who would traverse the dark pathways.'

Howard squirmed beneath Luke's frown, but took a breath, jutted out his chin and continued.

'The witching hour is the ideal time for rituals such as we must perform this evening; between three and four a.m., when the veil between worlds is at its thinnest. But as long as the sun is below the horizon we should be fine. There is a power in the moon which we must harness.'

'Harness?'

Luke's sardonic tone was unmistakeable.

'Sounds kinky. And are you adept at using these harnesses, Howard?'

Howard refused to allow Luke's crude inference to faze him.

'I have extensive experience...' he began, then his voice faltered. '... in the theories involved.'

'Theories. Brilliant.'

Luke rolled his eyes and strutted across the room.

'We're up against Voldemort, year seven, and I'm here with Ron Weasley, year one.'

Howard swallowed down the surge of inadequacy which threatened to undermine him. It was less his own skills which he doubted than his ability to convince Luke of the seriousness, the immense peril, of the task which lay ahead of them. Basic exorcism could be tricky enough, but evicting a demonic entity conjured a whole new set of challenges.

Personal interaction was Howard's failing, and Luke's barriers seemed to have been fortified even more strongly than they were only 24 hours previously.

'Are you... quite well, Master Kirkwood?'

'Master?'

Howard shrugged.

'Merely a term of deference to indicate—'

Luke cut him short.

'I know why you said it,' he snapped, 'but these aren't the 1920s and my father is dead, so I think *Mister* would be the correct form of address.'

Howard felt his face reddening and nodded his agreement.

'Of course, I didn't mean any—'

'But let's just stick with *Luke*, shall we?'

'Indeed,' Howard said. 'Luke.'

'And yes, I am "quite well", thank you.'

Howard sensed something dark, something hidden, behind Luke's eyes, beyond his words, but he was unable to interpret it.

'Now,' Luke said. 'Shall we press on?'

'Right, right, yes!'

Howard swung his case onto the desk, lining the base parallel to the edges of the leather inlay, then fiddled with the clasp, flipping the lid open. He took out the Magoralian Text, opening it at a marked passage and placing it carefully on the desk. Dark energy seemed to emanate from the book, sending a thrill through Howard's fingers as he stroked the page.

He lit the stub of a black candle with a lighter from his pocket and held a sage smudge stick over the flame until a wispy smoke curled up from the singed leaves. The smoke licked around his face and head and he inhaled deeply, stifling a small cough as the fumes tickled his throat. Holding the sage before him he paced to each corner of the room, whispering incantations under his breath, wafting the smoke over the walls and furnishings.

'Reminds me of Sunday roast,' Luke said, drawing Howard from his reverie.

'Ah, stuffing!'

Howard smiled and licked his lips.

Back at the desk Howard dropped the sage into a silver bowl and left it to burn out.

But for their own breaths and the gentle crackle of the flames in the bowl, the house was quiet and still.

Howard glanced towards the doorway.

'Will your mother be joining us?'

Luke's smile was stiff, forced.

'She's... lying down.'

Howard nodded.

'That's probably a good thing.'

'You think so?'

'There can be an element of danger involved in this kind of endeavour, Luke. Having to worry about the safety of a woman might hamper our concentration.'

The sneer Luke turned on him made Howard shudder.

'Well, despite your determination to adhere rigidly to that 1920s code of ethics, we certainly don't have to worry about my mother's safety.'

Luke broke the stare, turned away.

'Trust me,' he added.

Even with his slim understanding of social interactions Howard could sense the stress building within the young man, so he took no offence at his gruff manner.

'Very well,' he said.

Holding open the lapels of his jacket Howard offered an apologetic smile, as though removing his outerwear might offend his host, even though Luke was already in shirt-sleeves.

'Do you mind...?'

Luke glanced at him, shrugged.

'Make yourself at home.'

Howard shuddered, eyes flicking around the room. He had rarely felt less *at home.*

He slipped off the tweed and fitted it carefully on the back of the desk chair, adjusting the lie of the garment so that it hung smoothly. He unfolded a long black cloak from the case, shook it loose, then swung it around himself in a dramatic swirl, landing it with practiced elegance on his shoulders. He stood a moment, felt the effect, chin up, chest out.

Luke raised an eyebrow.

'Is that vital, or just for show?'

Howard coughed, hastily pulled off the cloak and flung it onto the chair over his jacket.

Luke held up a hand.

'Please,' he said, 'by all means, make yourself presentable.'

A shake of the little round head, eyes blinking behind the circular-framed spectacles.

'I can perhaps leave it until a little later.'

'Whatever,' Luke said.

His face took on a grim aspect as he marched to the desk, snatched open a drawer and took out a nasty-looking black pistol.

'Let's just get this sorted so we can bring that

bastard here and finish this for good.'

'Wh-what's that?'

Howard glared at the gun in horror.

'It may not be part of a wizard's bag of tricks,' Luke said, checking the magazine and slapping it back into the handle, 'but I'd have thought you'd recognise it.'

He cocked the firearm and tucked it into the back of his waistband.

'Where did you get it?'

Luke's laugh was cold and harsh.

'My father had a number of hiding places in this old house,' he said. 'And perhaps less faith in the occult than he led you to believe.'

Howard's hands wafted ineffectually.

'Conventional weapons are likely to have little influence upon the forces we are facing.'

'We'll just have to find out about that, won't we?'

Luke strutted across the room, Howard almost trotting to keep up.

'You might actually be adding to the peril before us,' Howard told him. 'Sorcery and bullets are a volatile mixture.'

'Sorcery?!' Luke snapped, turning on the smaller man, fire in his eyes. 'You've really bought into this madness, haven't you?'

'If you are so sceptical, why have you asked me back here today?'

An icy chill extinguished Luke's fiery gaze.

'You seemed like my best hope of a resolution to all this.'

'Even though you don't believe in magic?'

'Well...'

A non-committal shrug.

'Magic is real, Luke.'

'Yes?'

'Yes, very much so. Magic has existed as long as mankind has walked the Earth. Since the caveman's first breath of wonder at the diamond lights of the stars, strewn across the velvet blackness of the night sky. Drawing flames from the agitation of two pieces of wood elevated the early shaman above his mediocre brethren. Millennia later humanity believes there are no mysteries left to uncover, that science has disclosed all there is on this world and in space. But humanity is wrong, Luke. The mysteries still exist. The powers that seethe within the Earth, Moon, Fire and Sky are hidden, but no less real for all that.'

Howard's breathing quickened, his eyes appeared alight with the fire of his zeal.

'I have seen marvels such as you could not conceive, through windows that magic has opened into realms beyond our own universe, where impossible creatures that could not exist in our atmosphere or gravity roam free and vibrant. Sentient things with limbs beyond my counting. Things that crawl and things that climb. Things that fly and others that dig their way through the ground like worms, but are bigger than trains. Worlds of fire and worlds of ice. Worlds where the very air is toxic and corrosive, but the residents thrive there, even so. I've seen gateways higher than mountains, and dared not linger to see what came through. This existence that we cling to as being all and everything is but a fraction of what's out there. We are still those hairy brutes, Luke, watching sparks ignite from sticks rubbed together and scuttling away in alarm.'

Howard stood, chest heaving from the passion of his speech.

Luke regarded him silently, shaken by the sincerity in Howard's words, a new respect, almost awe, swelling inside him.

'Okay,' he murmured, after the longest time.

Howard cleared his throat, fiddled with his collar.

'Forgive me,' he said. 'It wasn't my intention to give a sermon.'

Luke waved away the apology.

'No, no, that was... enlightening. I'd never have thought. You seemed so...'

'What?'

Luke shook his head and gave what appeared to be his first genuine smile since Howard had arrived that evening.

'Never mind,' he said. 'Shall we begin?'

Howard clapped his hands eagerly.

'Yes, yes! Time is wasting.'

He unfastened his shirt cuffs and rolled up his sleeves.

Chapter Twenty

The surface of the desk was cluttered with items removed from Howard's voluminous case, such as black candles, a mortar and pestle, small bottles of herbs, amongst others. And a small stick of about 15 inches whittled from a gnarled and ancient branch of elder wood, one half bound in worn leather cord, the other stripped of bark and stained with natural dyes to a deep crimson hue. Howard reverently touched the wand and whispered a few words that Luke couldn't make out. A buzz of invisible energy tingled in Howard's fingers and he smiled, eyelids fluttering in an almost sensual manner.

Retrieving a stick of chalk from his jacket pocket Howard moved over to the big chair by the fireplace, grappling with the hefty object for a few seconds. A grunt of effort and a weary sigh.

'Do you mind...?'

Luke succumbed to the plea in his puppy-dog eyes. Between them they lifted the chair easily.

'Where do you want it?' Luke asked.

'Anywhere away from this spot.'

Howard nodded to the corner of the room and they manhandled the chair over there.

Hesitating over the space the chair had occupied Howard steeled himself before kneeling on the patch of discoloured floorboards. The eerie sensation emitted by the scorched wood froze the core of him. This was manifestly the locus of the breach, the existence of which he had theorised during his discussion with Luke's father.

Reaching out with the chalk he traced a wide arc on the floor, shuffling round on his knees until he completed a rough circle with an approximate diameter of four to five feet. He carefully ensured that the ends of the line met, and that the circle was whole and without breaks.

He felt Luke watching him intently.

'I presume this is acceptable? It's only chalk, it will clean away easily enough.'

The hitch of Luke's shoulders was becoming a familiar gesture.

'Certainly, whatever it takes. Washing the floor is the least of our worries.'

With a nod Howard bent to his task once more, drawing a five pointed star, each spiked tip reaching the circumference of the circle.

'Do we need to be naked?' Luke asked, out of nowhere.

Howard knelt up in alarm. Movies and popular fiction had ruined public perception of modern witchcraft, he feared.

'No!' he said. 'What you are wearing is fine.'

'Just wondered,' Luke said, with yet another shrug.

Howard shook off the disturbing image and, consulting his notebook, he chalked curiously shaped glyphs at each point of the pentacle. He tried to ignore Luke pacing, hands in pockets, sighing occasionally.

'Can I be doing anything?' the young man asked.

Howard put a final flourish to one of his esoteric designs.

'You could pour the whisky.'

'Whisky?' Luke scowled. 'I thought we were trying to get rid of this thing, not invite it for a party.'

'There's no question of a party,' Howard bristled. 'Such frivolities are far from my thoughts. It's merely a part of the ritual. There's a cup and a small bottle amongst my things.'

Luke rummaged through the muddle on the desk.

'Oh, yes,' Howard added, his mind already back on his task, 'and the cake.'

Howard missed Luke's expression of incredulity as he clambered to his feet and joined him at the desk.

Searching amongst his paraphernalia Howard found an egg-shaped lump of milky-white crystal which appeared to glow from within, its iridescent shimmer a result of light refracting on its unique composition, emitting a blueish sheen. Its touch reminded him of the first time he handled the moonstone, in Sri Lanka, when it was gifted to him by a beautiful, dusky-skinned Sinhalese witch girl whose smile made him blush.

He lifted the gemstone to his forehead, felt the cool energy at the point of his third eye, then moved to the window, lifting aside the heavy curtain.

The day had been dry after the downpour yesterday, and the night sky was clear, the stars stark and bright. A sliver of moon winked down at him. A full moon would have been preferable, but the timing was not of his choosing, and at least the cloud was sparse.

He held up the crystal in reverent offering, hand reaching between the thick iron bars, and spoke aloud, his voice a plaintive plea.

'Luna, Diana, Hecate, goddesses of the moon and night sky, bless us with the light of thy peace and wisdom, and grant us protection in what lies ahead.'

Turning back to the room he noticed the growing, if grudging, respect in Luke's eyes, and stood a little taller.

He waved the crystal over the objects on the desk, then replaced it carefully in a small, velvet pouch. He raised the cup of whisky and held it high.

'Bless this liquor, symbol of water and fire.'

He drank half the contents of the cup, coughing slightly as the fiery liquid seared his throat, then passed it to Luke, who downed the remains like water.

Luke had discovered a paper napkin parcel and unwrapped a portion of light, airy sponge cake which he passed to Howard.

Howard held the napkin out before him.

'Bless this food, symbol of earth and air.'

He broke the cake into two pieces and took one half for himself.

'Excuse fingers,' he said, popping his portion into his mouth.

Luke shrugged and ate the other half.

'Nice,' he said, mid-mastication. 'Did you bake this yourself?'

'No, it's Mr Kipling,' Howard said, brushing crumbs from his fingers, 'but it's just as effective for our purposes.'

'I'm sure it is,' Luke laughed.

But Howard wasn't smiling. His mind now focused on what was to come.

Taking the elder wand in his right hand and the Magoralian text in the left he faced the pentacle, taking a cautious step closer.

'*Maz sharat sha mashaz alamdak. Mushu maz sharat alash.*'

At first quietly, under his breath, then more loudly, more firmly with the repetition, Howard spoke the ancient phrase.

'*Maz sharat sha mashaz alamdak. Mushu maz sharat alash.*'

'I know those words,' Luke hissed, as if afraid to disturb whatever might be waiting in the shadows. 'What do they mean?'

Howard threw a reassuring smile over his shoulder.

'I'm just saying a friendly hello to our visitor. What was the name of that nightmare chap of yours?'

'You mean Mister Nice?'

'That's the fellow. Keep that name in your mind, Luke. Names have power.'

'But that name won't be any use for conjuring purposes,' Luke protested. 'It was just something I made up by mistake when I was eight years old.'

'On the contrary.'

Howard rested the old book on the mantelpiece. It was becoming heavy, and he felt he might need his hand free for what lay ahead.

'That name connects you to the being in this house,' he continued. 'It may be enough to get his attention, at the very least.'

'If you say so,' Luke said, and he began mumbling to himself. 'Mister Nice, Mister Nice.'

Howard flicked a few pages in the book, then propped the stub of a candle against it to keep his place.

'I've managed to unearth a number of names to use against our sinister guest. By matching the summoning spells used by your ancestor back in the day to the Book of Infernal Names, I think I have identified the creature who was called through from beyond.'

'You have?'

A note of hope quivered through Luke's response.

'Yes, so let us begin.'

Raising his hands in a grand gesture, wand wielded flamboyantly, Howard faced the circle once more. He took a deep breath and adjusted his stance, making ready to start.

Luke's words teased their way through his concentration.

'Do you want your cloak?'

Howard glanced at the chair where the cloak rested, tempted but not wishing to appear ridiculous in front of his host.

'I can manage.'

'It's okay if you do,' Luke encouraged.

It was clear Luke was as engaged in the ritual as Howard was.

Hesitating a moment longer, Howard's face softened into a shy smile.

'Go on, then.'

Luke fetched the cloak and helped Howard into it.

Suitably bedecked, Howard felt the surge of pride his ceremonial regalia endowed. Chin up, chest out, he began.

Chapter Twenty-One

'Jongruron, Thoz'gumath, Zal'gonoth... and Jack the Ripper!'

He heard the exclamation of surprise from the young man behind him, but before he could address it a sibilant whispering echoed those demonic names back at them, from the walls, from the ceiling, from all around, and Howard knew he must press on.

'By these names I call thee. By these names I summon thee. By these names I command thee!'

The bulbs in the chandelier flickered dramatically, the whispering intensified, the names snarled angrily, the echoes overlapping, chaotic and harsh.

Howard steeled himself, raised his own voice to combat the mayhem.

'Jongruron, Thoz'gumath, Zal'gonoth and Whitechapel Jack. By these names I bind thee!

A booming crash, like thunder, but not overhead in the cloudless sky, rather here in the very room with them. And a flare of light, bright as lightning, dazzling. One of the bulbs on the light fitting's outstretched limbs sparked and died. Howard and Luke both raised a hand to protect their eyes. Mist, or smoke as white as snow, swirled within the chalk circle.

Then, as eyes and ears recovered from the assault, a figure gradually emerged from the dissipating wispy fumes. Tall, strong, its clothes ragged, its countenance hideous, its demeanour menacing and oozing hatred.

It was unlike anything or any creature that

Howard had ever witnessed in all his explorations into the darkest realms, but he recognised it immediately.

Mister Nice.

Luke dropped to his knees as his childhood nightmares took corporeal form before him.

Howard took an involuntary step back, then swished his cloak, gritted his teeth and stared horror firmly in its yellow, glaring eyes.

'Jon...' he croaked, cleared his throat, began again. 'Jongruron, Thoz'gumath, Zal'gonoth and Whitechapel Jack. By these names I expel thee!'

The voices still snarled. The lights still flickered. And Mister Nice still stared back at him.

Howard's confidence faltered.

'Er, I expel thee,' he repeated tentatively. 'Begone, foul demon!'

The creature remained, monstrous features taunting.

'Begone, I say!'

Howard blinked, gulped.

'Why won't you begone?'

Mister Nice shuffled to the edge of the circle, waited a moment, then stepped beyond its chalk confines.

Howard's jaw hung in disbelief.

'But I binded thee. Er, bound thee. By your names. Jong... Um, Thoz... Jack?'

Mister Nice loomed closer, stiff, awkward, as if this form and its physical state were still unfamiliar to him. Towering over the terrified Howard he forced his raspy voice from inhuman lips.

'They ... are ... not ... my ... names.'

A slab-like hand clasped around Howard's neck.

The wand tumbled from his hand as he clawed in vain at the monster's clutching fingers. His eyes rolled back and his legs began to wilt beneath him.

Before his vision faded finally to black Luke's intervention brought blessed relief. The youth threw off his paralysis and hurled himself between the older man and the thing that held him, loosening the death grip. Howard tottered away, gasping.

Luke took up a stance in the space he had created, pulled the gun from his belt and pointed it at the creature.

Mister Nice merely returned his stare, making no attempt to defend himself. The howling of the voices and the erratic dancing of the lights escalated.

'We tried it your way, Howard,' Luke shouted above the din. 'Now let's try mine.'

'Luke,' Howard yelled. 'Get away from it.'

He grabbed Luke's sleeve to pull him clear but Luke shook him off.

'No! He's killed the only three people I loved in this whole shitty world, and now it's his turn.'

'But he's too powerful, you won't be able to...'

Then Luke's words filtered through his panicked state.

'Wait, three?'

'Father, Kaitlyn... and my mother.'

'But you said your mother was lying down.'

Luke risked tearing his eyes away from the monster's for a brief moment.

'She is,' he said. 'And has been since I found her cold body in that chair this morning.'

Howard gawped, agog.

'So you just...?'

'I couldn't involve the police, Howard. Not in

this madness. They couldn't help us. Mother would understand.'

The gun levelled on the creature's broad chest.

'This needs to end, now!'

'But the gun won't—'

Luke jerked the trigger. The loud report roared through the raucous maelstrom and a black hole appeared in the breast of the thing's ragged shirt.

But no blood flowed forth. The monster didn't fall, nor even stagger back or grimace in pain. It merely reached up a hand, twisted the gun from Luke's grip and tossed it aside. A swing of the creature's long arm sent Luke careering across the room, where he tumbled against the wing-backed chair in a daze.

Howard scrambled across to the fireplace, flicking through the pages of the book on the mantelpiece. He racked his brains, churning over the information he had gleaned since first opening this cursed volume, since Thomas Kirkwood had first pressed it into his hands. The names, the summoning spells... he felt sure he had worked it out correctly. It had to be him.

But the binding hadn't worked. The expulsion spell had failed disastrously. And now the creature lumbered towards him, grasping hands outstretched, malevolent eyes blazing.

'Who are you?' Howard demanded. 'If you're not the demon, who are you?'

As the steel rod fingers tightened on his frail flesh once more the fog finally cleared.

Across the room Luke struggled to his feet.

'Not the demon?' he gasped. 'Has all this been for nothing?'

With the last of his strength Howard pointed a

shaky hand towards the desk and the jumble of clutter accumulated there.

Luke rushed over, scrabbling through the items, discarding charms, candles, other occult trappings whose purpose he could only guess at, the constant noise and erratic lighting frustrating his efforts.

'What are you telling me, Howard?'

Howard's eyelids fluttered closed but his quivering hand still reached out.

Luke continued his search until his fingers fell on the dusty leather bindings of the journals which had sparked his father's interest, initiated his fatal journey of discovery. The journals written over a hundred years ago by their family's ancestor.

'Richard Kirkwood,' Luke croaked in shocked realisation.

Facing his oppressor, he raised his voice with conviction.

'Richard Kirkwood, by thy name I call thee!'

Mister Nice stiffened, releasing his limp victim. Howard slumped to the floorboards.

'By thy name I summon thee!'

Shuffling clumsily Mister Nice backed towards the chalk pentacle.

'By thy name I bind thee!'

The light in the room flared dazzlingly once more, a thunderous crash swallowed the chaotic tumble of sibilant voices. Then all was calm.

Silence now, and the remaining bulbs in the chandelier overhead glowed steady and bright.

In the circle Mister Nice was gone, replaced by a pale, hollow-faced man, his clothes shabby and worn, hair and flesh scorched and torn. He stood crooked, wretched, spears of hatred in his sunken eyes.

The sound of Howard's rasping breaths allowed Luke to breathe more easily.

'Well done, Luke,' came a voice seething with malice. 'I thought you would never make the connection.'

'What's all this about?' Luke asked. 'Why this charade? You've killed my family. *Your* family! How could you murder your own family?'

'Family?'

Richard Kirkwood's laugh was bitter and mocking.

'By name alone. After more than a century in torment do you imagine I would hesitate to spill Kirkwood blood because of a name?'

Kirkwood peered around his surroundings; the room, the desk, the walls and fireplace, tantalisingly familiar, teasing regretful memories. When next he spoke his tone held a note of contrition, almost apology.

'I was not always this way,' he said. 'Once I was foolish, idealistic. I believed in love and companionship... in whatever form.'

Was that shame which tinted those ashen cheeks?

'But people change. Circumstances change us. And our surroundings.'

All those years of torture and degradation oozed through his speech like the blackest treacle.

'We think we know what to expect from the black depths of Hades, swallowing biblical depictions of Hell and Damnation like children reading a storybook. Seas of flame through which we must crawl on our bellies, buzzards pecking at our eyes and delicate portions for untold eternities.'

His laugh rumbled with irony.

'But no, none of that. Hell is with us throughout our lives, hiding in the shadows and the flitting apparitions in the corners of our vision. It is born with us, grows with us, follows in every step we tread. Learning our fears. It is the worst of what we know in life, and more.

'Snatched from this earthly plane I plunged not into the blazing heat of hellfire, but rather into the bone-numbing chill of solitude. Vast, empty chambers echoing with no voice but my own. Yet from the corridor beyond came the shuffling of feet, the sibilant hiss of whispering. Was that Mother? Father? Had my wife sought me out, bringing my child to greet me? I had merely to fling open the door to discover them.

'But the heavy portals resisted my efforts. When finally I was able to cast them aside the halls beyond were bare and vacant, the voices stilled. Just darkness, emptiness, stretching out to the far, cavernous ceiling. But wait! There, beyond the next door, a noise, a voice. Someone, anyone, some companion to shatter this infinite loneliness. Through endless, maze-like corridors I chased phantoms, called out to shadows, never once receiving an answer.'

Kirkwood leaned closer, voice a hushed whisper, as if imparting a hard-earned truth.

'Hell is not fire and brimstone scorching our bodies and souls. It is hope, Luke. Hope, never dying but never fulfilled. An unbreaking cycle of desperation. So don't speak to me of family loyalties. My only priority was escape.'

Luke had been entranced, aghast. Now confusion twisted his face.

'Escape? How could you escape if you were dead?'

That laugh again, almost a growl, poisonous

and cruel.

'I wasn't dead, foolish boy. The demon dragged me to hell still alive, kept my heart beating all this time. It was only when you, a Kirkwood, blood of my blood, ruptured the barrier of death and came back alive that I found a way back through. I hid in your nightmares, fed them, watched them grow. But I needed the breach.'

'Breach?'

'The gateway I myself opened all those years ago, only to be snatched through it by my own ignorance and naivety. I needed your nightmares, and I needed the breach, but I needed them together.'

'You needed me to come here?'

'Indeed. Your father was quite selfish with this place, kept the family at arm's length. But once he was out of the way...'

Kirkwood stooped, tired and strained, but he lifted his chin and sneered.

'And tonight's little fiasco was a bonus I could not have foreseen. You threw me the lifeline I needed to scramble home.'

Luke shook his head, bewildered.

'But we didn't call you. We got the wrong names.'

'"Mister Nice, Mister Nice." Over and over in your fevered little brain. That's been my name for the past year.'

'Well, it won't do you any good,' Luke said, steadfast, defiant. 'You're still trapped.'

'Trapped?' Kirkwood drawled, smirking down at the chalk markings surrounding him. 'Here, in this cage for demons? Am I a demon, Luke?'

'What? I don't...'

Kirkwood stepped out of the circle.

Luke tried to move back, to make any movement at all, but found that he couldn't. he was stiff, immobile. His flesh and joints burned with agony.

'Oh, what's the matter, Luke?' Kirkwood mocked. 'Can't you move?'

Luke strained against the petrification, but in vain.

Kirkwood stalked unsteadily around Luke, bloodshot eyes evaluating.

'You're a fine, strapping boy, young Luke. Nice body. It'll look good on me.'

And Luke realised, as his blood turned to ice and his flesh became stone, Kaitlyn had never been Kirkwood's intended victim. Nor his mother. Not even his father. It was him. Always him.

Kirkwood ran a hand over Luke's cheek, his shoulder, down his arm, as if appraising his structure and physique, imagining himself wearing it, like a customer in a tailor's shop picking out a new suit.

'This ragged carcass I wear is being held together by strength of will alone. Your body is young and fresh...'

Howard Phillips, having heard all this, having watched all this through blurry eyes from his crumpled position on the tiled hearth, lurched to his feet, snatched the Book of Shadows from the mantelpiece and swung it, hard and fast, against the back of Richard Kirkwood's head. The crack of the impact resounded through the room.

Kirkwood tottered awkwardly, then spun around and swatted Howard aside.

But the damage was done, his attention distracted, the spell broken.

Luke jerked free of his paralysis, flexing his

regained limbs. He hurled himself at Kirkwood, grappling like a wrestler.

Luke was young and strong, but Kirkwood was sustained by sorcery and anger. They tumbled together across the room, staggering this way and that.

Howard watched, breath held behind gritted teeth.

'The circle, Luke,' he called. 'Force him back into the circle.'

Grunting and heaving the pair shifted slowly, inexorably towards the pentacle.

Howard retrieved his wand from the floor, spread his cloak impressively and waited for both combatants to enter the chalked circumference.

'Richard Kirkwood. Mister Nice,' he chanted, firm and proud. 'By these names, I expel thee!'

The flash flared once more, like sheet lightning filling the room, and the sonic boom loud enough to shock the senses. As Howard gradually regained his faculties he watched the figure of a young, strong man emerge from the kaleidoscopic blur, on hands and knees, chest heaving from exertion.

'Luke?' he whispered. 'Is it you?'

'Yes,' came the grateful reply. 'Yes, it's me.'

Relief sighed from the depths of Howard's soul as he strode over to help the boy to his feet.

Epilogue

Sunlight surging through the open curtains lent the study a bright, airy atmosphere it hadn't known in many years. Howard knelt, cloak returned to his case, sleeves rolled and a wet sponge in his hand, scrubbing the chalk markings from the floorboards.

His host stood by the window, watching the ambulance containing Emma Kirkwood's corpse as it drove off, soon disappearing beyond the boarded-up corner shop.

Howard looked up from his chore.

'What did the policeman say?' he asked.

'They'll want to see me again, after the post mortem, but they were remarkably understanding, given the circumstances.'

Howard nodded in grudging admiration.

'Richard Kirkwood was extremely careful to leave no trace of foul play.'

'Yes, wasn't he just.'

Howard bent back to his task.

'Be sure to obliterate that completely, won't you?' Luke instructed. 'I want no evidence that it ever existed.'

'Most certainly.'

Howard dunked the sponge in his bucket of soapy water.

'It'll be as if none of this ever happened.'

'Never happened?'

Howard blustered, horrified at his *faux pas*.

'Apart, of course, from your parents, and... I mean...'

Water dripped from his sponge and puddled

on the floor, soaking into the knees of his corduroy trousers.

He cleared his throat, face glowing crimson.

'Erm, will you stay here?' he asked. 'Keep the place on?'

'There's no need,' Luke said. 'It's influence has gone now.'

'Influence?'

'The hold this place had over me. Gone. All the way to Hell. Along with... him.'

Luke stared at the smeared chalk remnants.

Howard scrubbed harder.

'And good riddance, eh, Luke?'

He received no response.

'Luke?'

Luke faced the window again but his eyes were deep and distant. As Howard watched, Luke absently lifted a hand to his cheek, his shoulder, down his arm, in the manner of someone admiring the fit of a new suit, and cold uncertainty wrapped icy fingers around Howard's heart.

THE END...?

Printed in Great Britain
by Amazon

24259617R00116